Ashton Oxenden

My First Year in Canada

Ashton Oxenden

My First Year in Canada

ISBN/EAN: 9783337189945

Printed in Europe, USA, Canada, Australia, Japan

Cover: Foto ©Andreas Hilbeck / pixelio.de

More available books at **www.hansebooks.com**

MY FIRST YEAR IN CANADA.

BY THE

RIGHT REV. ASHTON OXENDEN, D.D.

BISHOP OF MONTREAL, AND METROPOLITAN OF CANADA.

𝔖𝔢𝔠𝔬𝔫𝔡 𝔗𝔥𝔬𝔲𝔰𝔞𝔫𝔡.

LONDON:

HATCHARDS, 187 PICCADILLY;

HAMILTON, ADAMS, AND CO. 32 PATERNOSTER ROW.

1871.

LONDON:
STRANGEWAYS AND WALDEN, PRINTERS,
Castle St. Leicester Sq.

CONTENTS.

MY FIRST YEAR IN CANADA.

CHAPTER I.

MY CALL TO CANADA.

IT has so happened that from failure of health, and other causes, I have visited many countries, France, Italy, Germany, Switzerland, Spain, Madeira, &c. But least of all did I think that I should ever set foot on the shores of the New World. God however sometimes selects a Home for us where we least expect it ; and certainly my present Home in Canada was not of my own choosing : God seemed to mark out the way for me, and called me hither.

The circumstances which led me to the Far West were these. One day in March, 1869, when my wife and I were passing a few days at Bournemouth, a Letter reached me, penned by a strange hand, and stamped with a foreign post-mark. Its contents too were as strange to me, and as foreign to my previous thoughts, as were the

B

Person who wrote it, and the quarter from whence it came.

The writer of the letter was a Canadian Bishop, who was at the time personally unknown to me. Its purport was to tell me that, in consequence of the lamented death of Bishop Fulford, the Synod of Montreal had met in the previous November, and had failed to accomplish its object, namely, the election of a Chief Pastor for the Diocese, and a Metropolitan of the Province of Canada. He informed me that the Synod would again meet in May, and asked if I would allow my name to be sent down by the Bishops, and whether, in the event of being elected, I should be content to fill the office.

After due consideration, and prayer to that Heavenly Counsellor on whose guiding hand I could unreservedly depend, and after consulting two confidential friends whose judgment I valued, I sat down to write my answer. It was, that for reasons which I mentioned, I felt myself unfitted for so high and onerous an office; and begged him not to submit my name as a candidate for the post. I despatched my letter, convinced that I had acted rightly, according to the best of my judgment, and feeling that I was in the hands of One who could and would overrule it, if He saw fit.

Nearly two months passed, and Montreal with

all the circumstances connected with it was almost forgotten; and certainly I never expected that my name would be even mentioned at the Synod after the decision I had come to, and which I had expressed in my letter. We were sitting at break- fast however one morning, in our sweet Kentish Rectory, when the postman brought my customary allowance of letters, and amongst them one with this startling address: 'The Rev. Ashton Oxenden, Bishop Elect of Montreal.'

I own it took me altogether by surprise. It informed me that my name had been duly suppressed by the assembled Bishops, in accordance with my wish, but that in the course of proceeding, circumstances arose which led to the mention of myself amongst that of others, by certain members of the Lower House; and eventually to my unanimous election.

Such were the contents of this most unexpected Letter from a friend then unknown to me, but whom I now regard as a beloved and valued Brother, the Bishop of Quebec.

What was to be done? I, of course, took counsel with my wife on a matter which so deeply concerned us both. To each of us our course seemed equally clear, and our duty plain; and never since has the conviction, on that day formed, once varied. Not one misgiving from that hour sprang up in our minds. A voice from above seemed to say, *Go;* and we had henceforth no doubt that such was the will of our Heavenly Father.

I will not weary my reader with all that occurred in quick succession during the next few weeks, and all the varied thoughts, which, flowing out as from a newly opened spring, rushed through our minds—the disclosure to our nearest friends of what had taken place, and of which they had not even a suspicion—the severance from a beloved flock, with whom I had been ministerially connected above twenty years—the rending of those family and social ties, which nature binds so strongly— the quitting a peaceful home and a beloved country —and the prospect of beginning life again in a new and unknown land. On these, both for my own and for my reader's sake, I refrain from dwelling.

Suffice it to say, that on Sunday, August 1st, 1869, I was consecrated in Westminster Abbey by the Archbishop of Canterbury and six assisting Bishops. And, having been thus solemnly set apart for my great and important work, I left the shores of England in the good ship 'Nestorian,' one of the fine Steamers on the Allan Line, com-manded by Captain Aird, of whom I cannot speak with too much praise. Our party consisted of my wife, myself, our child, and four faithful English maid-servants. After a speedy and prosperous voyage of ten days, we reached Quebec a little after midnight, on August 29th, a few hours before the dawn of a Canadian Sunday morning.

After a disturbed night's rest on board the Steamer, we rose, and were greeted by a kind deputation of Clerical brethren belonging to the city, and also of two Rural Deans of my Diocese, who had come all the way from Montreal to bid us a hearty and true welcome. We soon found ourselves at home among strangers: and after refreshing ourselves at a comfortable hotel (the St. Louis), we prepared for Morning Service at the Cathedral, where we and several of our fellow-passengers gave public thanks to God for the many mercies of a safe and successful voyage. I assisted in the service, and preached in the evening.

We were delighted with the striking situation and beauty of Quebec—a quaint old town, very foreign, and perched on the side of a steep hill, commanding a glorious view of the river and of the surrounding country. We remained there till the following evening, and then proceeded by rail to Montreal, a distance of 180 miles.

By the way, I must mention a curious incident that occurred. On the night of our arrival at Quebec, I had retired to rest in our little cabin, and had fallen asleep, in spite of the trampling of feet and other indescribable noises in the ship, all of which seemed to concentre at our door, and

were symptomatic of our having reached our port.
Presently a loud rap was heard; and after much
discussion on the outside, and a vain endeavour
on my part to persuade the people that I was only
half awake and did not wish to be disturbed, I
was told that Mr. B—— had sent his car, and
hoped I would make use of it. Who Mr. B——
was I did not know. I could only guess that he
was the proprietor of the hotel who had kindly
sent a conveyance for us; and so I begged to be
allowed to rest quietly where I was till morning.

A few minutes after came another knock. It
was in vain to close one's ears, or to refuse an
entrance. I was told that a Deputation was waiting to receive me. It was rather a trying hour
and place for so formal an interview; so I said
it was impossible, and still pleaded, as I had
done to Mr. B——'s messenger, a desire not to
be disturbed.

But to return to Mr. B—— and his Car. When
morning came, I learnt that Mr. B—— was not
only a leading member of our Church, but was
also a most important person at Montreal, on
whom the destinies of the railroad depended, and
one of the most intelligent, upright, and respected
men in Canada; and that the *Car* spoken of, and
which I in my English ignorance had mistaken
for a *Cab*, was his own private railway travelling-
carriage, which he had with very great courtesy

and kindness invited us to make use of. But he was too sensible and kind a person to be offended, and repeated his welcome offer for Monday evening; and in that comfortable and luxurious carriage, we (that is, our seven selves and our two Rural Deans) steamed on to Montreal, arriving there at eight o'clock on Tuesday morning.

Our journey from Quebec, though under most propitious circumstances, was somewhat tedious. The train was far less expeditious than those we had been accustomed to in England, and the stoppages seemed to be needlessly protracted. The Grand Trunk is making rapid improvements; but still there is a lack of that smartness and regularity, which are met with on English lines. The stations are miserable; and there are no porters to help the passengers on their arrival, but each one is expected to shift for himself as best he can. I must say however that in my various railway trips, I have met, from officials and others, with as much courtesy and attention as could possibly be shown in any country.

The luggage system is well managed, and it is scarcely possible for any one to lose his baggage. Its safety is ensured by checks, given to the possessor, with corresponding numbers attached to the goods themselves. As a single line generally prevails in Canada, the trains are necessarily few and far between. The carriages, or cars, are long narrow conveyances, resembling in some respects our second-class compartments, but far more comfortable. There are only two grades of conveyance ; the one in which the world in general travels, and the other which is only resorted to by those to whom cheapness is an object. In addition however to these, a new description of car has been introduced upon some of the lines, luxuriously furnished, and provided with every comfort for a night journey.

But to go back to our journey from Quebec. At St. Hilaire, Major C——, who is the possessor of one of the old Seigneuries, a warm-hearted Englishman, and a staunch friend of the Church, joined us, bidding us welcome to the neighbourhood of Montreal. On arriving at the Bonaventure Terminus, a large number of Clergy, with the venerable Dean at their head, were assembled to receive us; and with them were the leading Laymen of the city and neighbourhood. Their welcome was very touching, making us feel at once that we had come among friends, and that our new abode would soon prove a home to us.

The various introductions over, we drove up in Mrs. H——'s carriage, with the Dean and Mr. Hutton (the Diocesan Treasurer), to our residence in Drummond Street, which had been generously provided for us free of expense for the next eight months. Here we found every want anticipated, and every comfort supplied. The urn was even fizzing on the table, a delicious breakfast ready, and our larder and storeroom filled for weeks to come. I never ate a meal with feelings of greater thankfulness.

On the afternoon of the same day, an Address was presented to me in the Synod room from a large gathering of the leading Laymen, and another on the next day from the Clergy. These were followed by others — by the English Working Men's Society, and a week later by the Bishops of the Province, who were represented in person by the Bishops of Quebec and Huron, who had kindly travelled many miles to express their hearty welcome.

During the first few days we had little time to ourselves, for besides my more public engagements, our visitors vied with one another in testifying their hearty goodwill and kindness to us. Our hearts must have been dull indeed, if we could have mistaken these tokens of affection so sincerely offered to us.

On the first Sunday after our arrival, September 5th (having previously re-appointed as my chaplains the two clergymen who had filled that office under my predecessor), I was duly installed in the Cathedral, a building erected nine years ago, and of great beauty, worthy of the Metropolitan See of Canada. At the close of the service,

I preached on the text,* 'Whom shall I send, and who will go for us ? Here am I, Lord, send me.' I also preached in the evening to a large and attentive congregation.

And here ended the more public ceremonies connected with my entrance upon Episcopal life in Montreal—a life which I humbly trust may in some measure tend to the promotion of my Master's kingdom and glory.

* The Sermon is given in the Appendix.

CHAPTER II.

FIRST IMPRESSIONS OF MONTREAL.

OUR first impressions of the city of Montreal were very favourable. It is a well-built town, beautifully situated on rising ground, and backed by a fine mountain-like hill, from which it takes its name (Mont Real), having at its foot the huge and noble St. Lawrence. It has been justly called ' The young and beautiful Queen of the West.'

The lower parts of the town, near the river, are chiefly inhabited by the French-speaking portion of the population, with the exception of two or three leading streets filled with first-rate shops, which are mostly served by English proprietors ; and still nearer the river are clustered the handsome warehouses and offices of our wealthy merchants. The upper parts of the town are of more recent growth, and contain commodious and detached houses, belonging to men of business and persons of fortune. The streets in this part of the town are as yet incomplete, showing at present certain gaps, which will ere long be filled up with handsome houses. They are all flanked by trees,

chiefly maples, which, besides the welcome shade
they afford in summer, greatly add to the beauty
of the town.

One thing particularly struck us at first, namely,
that most of the houses have their shutters closed,
so that the rooms are in almost funereal darkness.
This arises from the necessity in hot weather of
excluding the burning sun, and also the flies which
here abound.   And the consequence is that people
get so used to this state of things, that darkness
becomes the normal condition of many rooms
even in winter.   Loving as I do the bright sun-
shine, it will be long before I shall be prepared
to endorse this custom.

The Montreal builders are excellent.   They not
only run up their houses at an indescribable speed,
but they build them well and substantially.   A
house begun in the early spring is often finished, and
even inhabited, before the following winter.   The
exceeding dryness of the climate facilitates this
speedy occupation.   The English maxim does not
therefore hold good in this country, 'When your
house is built you should put your enemy into it
the first year, then your friend, and afterwards you
may get into it yourself.'   We are now building a
house under the wing of the Cathedral for the
Bishop's residence;   but we are too fresh from
England to hurry matters; and so, having begun
it in April, it will be finished in the spring, and we

hope to get into it next autumn. I was unwilling to have entered upon this responsibility, since it involves a permanent tax upon the episcopal income; but a small sum originally devoted to the purpose was available to meet about one-third of the outlay, and it seemed to me especially desirable to do something towards the completion of the group of ecclesiastical buildings around our beautiful Cathedral. May it be the peaceful and happy abode of many of my successors! I cannot expect it to be more than a very temporary residence for myself.

I cannot speak with much praise of the street roads of Montreal. This year, at least, they have been in a chronic state of roughness, and the consequent jolting is extremely unpleasant. It must be very difficult however to keep them in decent repair, in consequence of the severity of the winter, with its repeated attacks of frost and snow. The side-walks are not paved, but are covered with strong springy boards, which, though somewhat unsightly, are by no means unpleasant to walk upon.

The streets are all alive with carriages, both hired and private, and the pace at which people drive is at first rather alarming to a sober, slow-moving Englishman. The public cabs have a very old-fashioned look, being very high from the ground and difficult of entrance, with a good deal of silver about them, and of the stamp of the Louis Quatorze age.   They are however very clean, and the drivers are generally honest and unexacting.

The private carriages are extremely well appointed.   They are well built, and the horses good; but one misses the neat liveries to which we are accustomed in England; and the practice which prevails pretty generally of driving with one rein in each hand, strikes one as being a little awkward.

The chief buildings which adorn the city of Montreal are its Churches.   The largest, although not the most beautiful, are the Roman Catholic Church of Notre Dame, and the Jesuits' Church in Bleury Street.   But the English Churches are far more beautiful, at least to our taste.   Of these our Cathedral stands first and foremost, being a large cruciform building, and a very pure specimen of the Early Decorated style of Gothic architecture, with a simple but extremely beautiful little Chapter-house beneath its shadow.

The whole is very chaste and handsome.   The inside is less effective than the exterior.   The recent addition of an obelisk to the memory of the late Bishop makes the group complete.

Besides the Ecclesiastical buildings, there are others which strike the eye.   M'Gill College is admirably placed with the mountain as a background, and a little park in front.   It is a secular

University, and well managed. Then the principal Banks, St. Patrick's Hall, the Town Hall, &c. are all worthy of this flourishing and wealthy city.

The Victoria Bridge, which spans the broad St. Lawrence, is one of the wonders of Canada. This enormous bridge is, I believe, nearly two miles long. It is of wrought-iron, and rests upon twenty-four limestone piers. The railway passes over it, and it is therefore of immense importance to Montreal, and to Canada generally. It was constructed at an expense of about one million and a half sterling.

Montreal has lately sustained a great loss in the removal of the Imperial troops. The barracks have now a deserted look, and I fear that very soon there will not be a soldier left.

At one time it was doubtful whether Montreal would not be chosen as the Seat of Government. In many respects it seemed the obvious place for this distinction ; but for reasons, wise or unwise, Montreal was set aside, and Ottawa chosen. In the latter city Government buildings have been erected on a large and splendid scale ; and there the Governor-General resides at Rideau Hall, just outside the town ; and there also the Dominion Parliament meets, and the Ministers of State have their offices.

The Parliament consists of an Upper House, or Senate, chosen by the Crown, and a Lower House elected by the people. The members of the former have the title of 'Honourable' prefixed to their names for life. The same privilege belongs to those who have served as Ministers of State.

The city of Montreal has a Mayor and Corporation, to whom is entrusted the management of its local concerns. The inhabitants are exceedingly well conducted. One rarely meets with anything that offends either the ear or the eye, and a drunkard or a beggar is seldom seen; on Sunday too the streets are unusually quiet and orderly.

Upon the whole, I prefer Montreal, as a place of residence, to almost any town that I have ever seen. And we may truly feel that 'our lines are fallen in pleasant places,' and that God has surrounded us with temporal blessings far beyond our deserts.

But the loveliest spot does not constitute happiness. Our joy depends far more on *what* we are than *where* we are. A right and well-regulated mind is a better possession than the most favoured dwelling-place.

CHAPTER III.

VISITATIONS ABOUT THE DIOCESE.

MY first purely episcopal act was the consecration of the pretty little church at Como, a hamlet on the south bank of the Ottawa. This took place just a fortnight after our arrival in Canada.

The morning was lovely, though somewhat hazy. Our party, which numbered eight or ten, consisted of my wife and myself, my chaplain Mr. L——, two other clergymen, their wives, and the Archdeacon of Ontario, who joined us on the way. We left Montreal by train for Lachine, where we took the steamer, and at twelve o'clock arrived at Como. We had been detained for nearly two hours by a river fog, and found the congregation waiting for us. The church is small, but very pretty, and in good taste. It is situated in a picturesque and peaceful spot near the river. The congregation was not large, but devout and orderly; and all seemed to enter warmly into our simple but beautiful Consecration Service. We afterwards, all of us, assembled at Mr. G——'s house on the banks of the river. It was a happy

day for us, and a still happier perhaps for our good
and generous hosts, through whose exertions, and
that of their neighbours, the little church had been
erected.

Not one of our party was allowed to pay either
for our voyage, or for our journey by rail. Such
is the liberality one meets with in this country.

A week later, I went a little higher up the
river, being anxious to seize the opportunity of
fine weather for visiting this portion of my
Diocese.

The Ottawa runs from north-west to south-east,
uniting itself with the great St. Lawrence a few miles
above Lachine. It is a splendid river of considerable
width, but the navigation is occasionally impeded
by rapids, so that the steamboat here and there
leaves the river for a few miles of rail, or for a
short canal. The scenery is generally picturesque,
without reaching the standard of beauty : it lacks
boldness and diversity of character. In the autumn
however there is one feature peculiar to Canada, and
very apparent here, namely, the crimson tint of
the foliage. This effect is principally produced by
the leaf of the maple-tree, which turns to a deeper
and more vivid red than even our own Virginian
Creeper.

But the maple-tree, which abounds in this
country, has another excellency. It produces in
the spring a valuable sugar, which exudes from the

tree when tapped, and is much used in Canada.
The maple sugar-season is quite an epoch in the
year. It occurs in the early spring, when the first
warm weather causes the sap to rise. An incision
is then made in the bark, and the bleeding of the
tree takes place. To make this operation perfectly successful, two or three morning frosts are
needed at this crisis, which greatly facilitate the
flow of sugar, and improve its taste. The fluid is
boiled, and afterwards becomes solid, in which state
it is mostly used ; but it also makes a very pure
and agreeable syrup.

But to return to my Visitation tour. It was but
a short one this time, and I was quite alone. My
first point was St. Andrews, a village on the opposite side to Como, being the principal parish in this
part of the Diocese, from which the Deanery bor-
rows its name.

At starting the day was wet, and I spent my
time on board the steamer in preparing my sermon
for the Cathedral on the following Sunday. We
passed Como, which certainly had a less *riant*
appearance than it had a week ago, caught a
glimpse of the little church which will be ever dear
to me as being the first-fruits of my Episcopal
office, and reached St. Andrews about one o'clock.
This place is only two miles distant from the river,
and is one of the seven Rectories in the Diocese,
constituted by royal patent.

The worthy rector, Mr. L——, is the rural dean.
A service was held that evening in his church, and,
in spite of bad weather, about a hundred and
thirty persons were present, and I preached to
attentive hearers.

Next morning, after breakfast, Mr. L—— drove
me along a roughish road to Grenville; I enjoyed
my drive, though it was none of the smoothest. The
constant glimpses of the Ottawa were very pretty,
and my companion extremely agreeable.

At Grenville we had Service on our arrival, and
slept at the parsonage, the owner of which, Mr.
N——, is brother to one of my old Pluckley
parishioners.

At these Parsonages, which are less luxurious
than those in England, one always meets with a
most kind and warm reception. The clergy have
usually but a very limited income, seldom exceeding 600 dollars, or 120*l.* sterling, and often
less. Frequently their household concerns are
carried on without the aid of a servant; and even
the horse, which is a needful appendage to a
missionary's establishment, is looked after by the
clergyman himself, or one of his family.

After a short drive to the river, I proceeded
alone by steamer to Ottawa. This mode of travelling is very agreeable both in good and bad
weather. The vessels are clean, roomy, and convenient. The meals on board are nicely managed,

and the food excellent. The proprietors and officials moreover are unusually civil and obliging. All this makes a day on board a pleasure instead of a weariness.

We arrived late at Ottawa, where I was received by Mr. J——, the Incumbent of Hull, which is in my Diocese, whereas Ottawa itself is in the Diocese of Ontario. There was a room full of ladies and gentlemen in the evening to meet me.

The next morning there was Service at eleven o'clock at Hull. The little church is one of the prettiest in Canada, new and in excellent taste. There was a good congregation and a nice warm service. I preached as usual. We then returned to Ottawa, dined, and walked out to see the Houses of Parliament.

Ottawa is strikingly situated on a rocky eminence, overhanging the river. The new Government buildings which crown the hill are a beautiful and substantial group, lately erected at a vast expense. The town itself is poor and unfinished. Indeed it will take years before it can present an appearance worthy of its position as the seat of the Dominion Government.

In the afternoon Mr. J—— drove me to Aylmer, a distance of eight miles, along an excellent road. Here, again, a Service had been announced, and a fair congregation was assembled. Mr. S——, the

incumbent, is a St. Augustine's man.   After service
we drove back to Ottawa, had some tea, and went
to bed.

At six o'clock next morning I was on board
my favourite steamer on my return to Montreal,
which I reached about five o'clock, having passed
five very successful days.

After a day's rest at Montreal, and preaching
at the Cathedral, I started again on Monday,
September 27th, on another short Confirmation
tour with my chaplain, Mr. L——.   The weather
had become cold, and I was not feeling very well.
The first place we visited was Hemmingford, which
we reached by train, thirty miles from Montreal;
and there the rural dean, Mr. D——, met us and
joined us in our tour.   The incumbent, Mr. M——,
was a young deacon who had formerly belonged
to the Presbyterian Church.   An open log-fire, a
rather unusual luxury, greeted us on our arrival.
This was no small comfort, and around it we
gathered gladly.   At night I suffered a great deal
from the sudden change of the weather; for it had
become exceedingly cold.

The Church was half a mile off, and thither we
repaired in the morning, and found a good congregation, and twenty-five candidates.   This was my
first opportunity of performing the rite of Confirmation.   I addressed them for a few minutes

before the laying on of hands; and then invited
the congregation to join me in silent prayer. I
confirmed each one singly, coming up one by one,
which had a solemn effect. And I then preached
from St. Matthew, ix. 9. There was also an Adult
Baptism, which was very striking in its connexion
with Confirmation, and preparatory to it.

It was my birthday, and I was greatly interested
in this my first Confirmation, which I conducted
ever after on nearly the same plan—addressing
the candidates for five minutes before the question
is put—having a very short, silent prayer—laying
hands on each severally—and then, when the service is completed, preaching an unwritten sermon
to the congregation generally, but more pointedly
to the confirmed.

After service, Mr. D—— drove me fifteen miles
to Russel town, where I slept. I was very cold,
but they kindly put up the winter stove, and made
a fire in my bedroom.

Next morning there was a Service at ten at
Havelock, one of Mr. F——'s churches, and twenty-
five candidates. At Franklin, four miles on, we had
a second service, but no Confirmation; and I consecrated the Burial-ground. We then returned to
Mr. F——'s house, where I passed a second night.

We proceeded in the morning to Hinchingbrook. The road was considered to be a good
one, but I thought it very rough; and it certainly

tried the springs of our waggon and the strength of my back. At Hinchingbrook we had service, with twelve candidates—the congregation small.

Another kind person drove us on to Huntingdon for afternoon Service. The readiness with which one is driven from place to place is very striking. No difficulty is ever raised, and no one seems to grudge the use of his carriage if he possesses one, but it is forthcoming as a matter of course ; and I have never on any tour found it necessary to hire a conveyance. It does indeed compensate for many inconveniences to meet with such invariable and freely offered goodwill on the part of both clergy and laity.

At Huntingdon I found a nice little parsonage-house, furnished with great taste and comfort by Mr. and Mrs. E -—. And here we had a crammed Church and thirty-five candidates. Two ladies had come from the States, twenty-five miles off, having read some of my books. A few of the leading parishioners assembled at the parsonage in the evening.

The next day was the close of my present tour. About ten miles brought us to Durham, where we had a Confirmation at ten, in a tolerably filled church. There were twenty-seven candidates. After refreshing us with dinner, Mr. B——, the incumbent, kindly drove us twenty-five miles along a jolting road to the Indian village of

Caughnawaga, from which we crossed the Ottawa, and reached home late at night. Our drive, though rough and long, was pleasant. It was over a good deal of what is called *corduroy* road, that is to say, a road formed by trees laid across as the foundation. This causes constant ridges like corduroy cloth, and there is a perpetual bumping, which cannot be avoided. Occasional holes in the road are bad enough; but these unseen furrows, which are just concealed by the mud, are still more dislocating.

Thus ended very happily my first Confirmation Tour. All was new to me, the services, the country, the mode of travelling, &c. But I was most thankful to have accomplished it, and not a little rejoiced to reach home and find all well, and myself none the worse for my journey and labours.

After the refreshment of a quiet Sunday, and preaching at St. Stephen's to a crowded congregation, I went next day, October the 4th, by the four o'clock train to Lacolle, a distance of forty miles, where Mr. L—— met me and took me to his parsonage. At one of the stations at which we stopped, a very old man, with silvery hair, came into the railway-carriage, lantern in hand, and asking me if I was the 'Lord Bishop,' he said he had come to welcome me, having been himself eighty years in Canada. These little traits of courtesy and goodwill are something more than mere formalities, and are cheering to a new comer into a strange land.

Next morning we had our Confirmation service, and eighteen candidates, with a fair congregation, considering a deluge of rain. The evening train having been taken off, I was detained a second night at Lacolle.

I returned to Montreal for a few hours, and was off again in the afternoon for St. Remi. The parsonage being at a distance from the station, I was entertained by Mr. D——, a wealthy farmer of the place, who, with his wife, showed me true kindness and hospitality, inviting three or four of their neighbours to meet me in the evening.

The next morning, Mr. S——, the clergyman, drove me to his little church (the smallest in the Diocese), where we had a thin congregation, and only two candidates. We then went on to the parsonage, which was close to Mr. S——'s second church, where we had an afternoon service and fourteen candidates. I returned to Montreal the same evening, and reached my home at eleven o'clock, very tired. The rough roads, constant change of quarters, &c. are rather trying ; but all these are nothing when one is in the pleasant path of duty, and engaged in the service of a loving Master.

CHAPTER IV.

A VISITATION TOUR HIGHER UP THE OTTAWA.

ON the day after my return from St. Remi, Oct. 9th, an event took place which caused a great sensation among the community of Montreal—the arrival of H.R.H. Prince Arthur, who had come to join his regiment, the Rifle Brigade, and to spend the winter in Canada. He was enthusiastically welcomed by the Mayor and Corporation, and conducted to his residence amidst general rejoicing. I asked permission to pay my respects to him on the following day with the Dean, when we were graciously received by him.

I may truly say that no person ever created more interest, made fewer enemies, and more real friends, than our young English Prince. The unselfishness of his character, his desire to please, which was unceasing and not forced, the invariable uprightness of his conduct, his happy way of doing and saying always the right thing, made his presence like a sunbeam among us, and produced great happiness wherever he went. Both he and his suite made an impression during their stay in

Montreal which will never be effaced. In his household there was no display; but a quiet, refined, and royal tone pervaded the whole of the arrangements.

The next day, Saturday, I had a whole holiday. On Sunday I preached at the Cathedral and at St. James's; and on Monday, October 11th, I left home with my wife on another expedition up the Ottawa, with a view of going higher up the river this time, and visiting three stations at the further extent of my Diocese to the north-east.

The day was delightful, the tints most lovely, and the steamer very comfortable. My good friend, Mr. L——, the rural dean, joined us at Carillon, and remained with us for four days. We reached Ottawa in the evening, but pushed on to Aylmer, where we slept, as the Upper Ottawa boat starts from thence.

Tuesday, October 12th, we left at seven for Onslow; but to our dismay, instead of finding a nice, clean, comfortable vessel, we had to put up with a dirty little tug-boat, rigged out for the occasion, as the regular packet was undergoing a thorough refitting for Prince Arthur, who was expected in these parts in a day or two. This detracted somewhat from the comfort of our voyage.

When on the Ottawa the scene is often enlivened by the appearance of a huge raft which comes in sight. These rafts bring down the sawn timber from the mills at Ottawa and elsewhere, which is eventually shipped either for England or for the United States. They are of an enormous size, and are composed of timber bound together by clamps of wood into a solid stage, and generally so constructed as to be subdivided into two or three compartments, in case of a storm. On one of these rafts are sometimes erected four or five wooden houses, the dwellings of the raftsmen. These floating islands drop down the stream, and are guided by long oars. The lumber of which they are composed has probably travelled some hundred miles from the forest in the interior.

The life of the shanty-men, who fell the timber, is a very peculiar one. Being engaged by the lumber merchants, they go up in the month of October or November in regular gangs to certain localities in the Bush, previously untrodden by the feet of men. There they establish themselves during the long winter ; and the trees which they fell are dragged out over the snow by oxen or horses, and then floated down the river to the saw-mills.

These hardy men meet with many privations ; but they live well, having plenty of good beef and pork to support them. They are restricted, however, from the use of spirits, and indulge in no stronger drink than tea, with an abundance of which they are liberally supplied; and the quality, I am told, is excellent.

The shanties are temporary wooden buildings, each one holding from twenty to thirty persons. They are divided into two compartments—the one for cooking, and the other for eating and sleeping; the latter being usually furnished with two tiers of berths.

An occasional Missionary visits these shanties, attracted there by a desire to carry the glad and welcome tidings of the Gospel; and if he comes in a right spirit, he is pretty sure to meet with a kind and warm reception. Three of our Clergy have volunteered to devote a week or two to this self-denying service in the coming winter. But I hope the time will come when our Church will be able to employ two regular travelling Missionaries, whose time shall be entirely occupied in going from shanty to shanty during the winter months. We need special funds for the purpose; but I cannot help trusting that the means will be supplied for so blessed an object.

We landed at Onslow about ten o'clock, a pretty missionary station amidst the woods. The clergyman was Mr. B——, who had visited us at Pluckley before leaving England. He and a brother clergyman received us at the landing-place, and drove us to the parsonage. Service was at three o'clock, but rain had come on, and greatly thinned our congregation. There were only five candidates. On the same evening we had a Missionary Meeting at seven o'clock.

These missionary meetings are very unlike ours in England. In the first place, they are usually held in the Churches, for want of room elsewhere. And then the object is not so much missionary work among the heathen, as the support of the Church in the Diocese. This causes a little flatness, and a lack of that stirring life and interest, which marks some of our Parish missionary gatherings at home. I cannot but think that our Church in Canada, needy as she is, would have a larger blessing if she did more for our brethren in distant lands.

We left next morning early, October 13th, in Mr. R——'s waggon for Clarendon, a distance of sixteen miles. The drive interested us a good deal, as the scene was new to us, the country through which we passed being only half cleared. Of this kind of country we have had many specimens since. We passed through some miles of pure Bush or natural wood-land, the trees being chiefly maple, pine, ash, and hemlock, the bark of which latter is greatly used here for tanning purposes. Then at intervals we came to an open space with a Log House erected in it by some recent settler. The clearances are made either by cutting down the trees, or, more commonly, by burning them. But the stumps are allowed to remain about three feet above the ground, presenting the appearance of a huge graveyard. The custom is to leave these stumps for several years till they are fairly rotted, as the expense of grubbing them in their sound state would be ruinous. My wife much enjoyed the drive, and I should have enjoyed it too, for our friends were very pleasant and agreeable, and we had two good horses which carried us along famously, but I was a little out of order, and the morning was chilly. Halfway however we got my indian-rubber foot-warmer filled at a cottage, which nearly set me right again.

When we arrived at Clarendon, the Church-bell had been ringing for some little time, and the people were all assembled for service. The church has little to recommend it ; but the largeness and earnestness of the congregation made up for all that was wanting, and our hearts were warmed and our spirits cheered by the hearty service. Fifty-two were presented for Confirmation, several of whom were grown-up persons; and this is often the case in Canada.

In the evening we had a Missionary Meeting, which partook of the same character as that on the previous evening. In each case the Clergy were all in surplices, and spoke from the Chancel.

October 14.—Off at nine o'clock for Portage du Fort. A 'Portage' is, properly speaking, a road by the river's side, where there is a rapid. But it is often used, I believe, for other roads as well. Our party had now swelled to the number of ten persons, namely, my wife and self, Mr. and Mrs. R—— and others of their family, Mr. L——, our rural dean, and Mr. K——, a clergyman from Thorne. An agreeable drive through a half-cleared country, much like that of yesterday, brought us to Portage du Fort. Here again the people were all assembled, but the congregation was small. There were thirteen candidates for Confirmation. It was rather a mixed service, as I had appointed the day as a general Harvest Thanksgiving day throughout the Diocese before I had arranged my Visitation tour. This interfered somewhat with the distinctness of the service. Mr. G——, I grieve to say, has since left the parish and Diocese for a post in the States.

Soon after daybreak our kind host and hostess, and the rural dean, walked down with us to the river, and there left us on board our steamer. Again we had to put up with an inferior boat, the regular one being detained for the Prince, who had meanwhile gone a little higher up the river. But our Captain was most civil and obliging, and gave us up his nice airy cabin on deck, which was a refreshing change from the saloon below. A part of this journey was performed in a somewhat novel manner. Half-way between Portage and Onslow is a rapid over which the steamer

cannot pass.   This interval is supplied by a
wooden railway.   Over this line, which is three
miles long, we were drawn by two horses tandem.
In portions of it, the little railway spans a deep
ravine, and as there is no parapet fence, it was
rather a strain upon one's nerves.   However they
assured us that never yet had a single accident
occurred ; and so we were content.

On reaching Aylmer, Mr. J—— met us, and
drove us to his house at Ottawa.   As however
we were to make an early start on the following
morning, we thought it wiser to sleep on board,
and were quite glad to find ourselves once more
in our favourite steamer.   The next day we de-
scended the river, and reached home in good time
the same evening.

Our trip had now come to a happy close, and
it was time that we should cease our travellings
for the present year.   The weather was fine, but it
had become cold, and there was a taste of autumn
in the air.

It is clear that more Clergymen are needed
in the district of the Upper Ottawa.   The present
staff is overtaxed, and is not sufficient to occupy
the ground open to us, and these few are miserably
paid.   Additional men are wanted, and more
money.   I am determined, if possible, to obtain the
latter, and God will, I believe, provide the former
to meet our requirements.

I made with my wife yet one more excursion, and then we shut up for the winter. This was to Dunham, where I was anxious to attend a Ruri-decanal meeting.

We started on Saturday, October 23rd, in a torrent of rain from the Montreal station for Stanbridge, where Mr. S——, the rural dean, sent his brougham to meet us, a luxurious mode of conveyance not often met with here.   But, alas, we discovered, on leaving the train, that our luggage had been left behind at St. John's! And how could a Bishop show himself on Sunday without his Episcopal attire? There was no other train due before Monday morning.   However we telegraphed ; and fortune favoured us, for there happened to be a special freight train just starting, which brought us our lost luggage, and gladdened our hearts.   I preached at Bedford in the morning, and at Frelighsburg, ten miles off, in the evening, sleeping at Mr. D——'s rectory.

Next morning, 25th, we went on to Dunham, where about twenty clergymen were assembled, and fourteen churchwardens. The meeting took place in the underground basement of the church, which was warmed nearly to boiling heat. The Rural Dean was in the chair. The meeting lasted about three hours, when we adjourned for tea and evening service.

There was vigour in this meeting, and more

than an average measure of intelligence, but a
painful lack of gentleness and moderation among
the speakers, which marred its effect.   In the
evening I preached on the love of Christ.   There
was a church full of people, and the service was
very calming.

I woke next morning with a terrible cold,
which had been coming on for some days.   This
was not improved by the snow which we found
upon the ground on looking out of our window,
nor by an early walk to church, where we received
the Holy Communion together.   This however was
a blessed preparation for our adjourned meeting
after breakfast, when a much better spirit showed
itself, and such a Christian tone as made me leave
Dunham with feelings of thankfulness.   We returned to Bedford, had some tea at Mr. S——'s,
and got home to Montreal by ten o'clock.

The chief subjects discussed at the meeting
were the mode of raising funds for our Church
work, and the best means of dealing with the
younger members of our body, which latter subject led to the formation of an organised Church
Association for the various parishes in the diocese.

The Ruri-decanal system was also a subject
that cropped up two or three times at the meeting.
I find the office of Rural Dean somewhat unpopular
in the Diocese, and especially in these parts.   But
being an important organisation in the Church, and

one that is likely to be very helpful to myself, I feel unwilling hastily to abandon it. I have therefore somewhat modified the system by requesting the clergy in the several deaneries to nominate for my approval one of their own choice, and also by limiting the term of office to three years, and, further, by carefully defining the rural dean's powers. With these changes I trust that the system will yet work well, and prove useful in the Diocese. It is surely very important that any changes which may be needful in the various missions should pass through the local board of the deanery, and receive their sanction, before being finally adopted; and if a rural deanery is necessary, there must be an officer at the head of it.

Though pleased with our visit to the eastern townships, we were thankful to get home, for there was a decided change in the weather, and it was time to get into our winter shell. If the reader has grown tired of my travels, he may console himself by knowing that I was fairly tired out also.

CHAPTER V.

SHORT TRIPS IN COLD WEATHER.

DURING November, and the five following months, I considered myself debarred from regular Visitations in the Diocese on account of the weather. I was able however to make an occasional short expedition, and chiefly by railroad.

One of them was a visit to Chambly, where Mr. W——, who had been my fellow-labourer at Pluckley up to the time of my coming out to Canada, had lately accepted a post; and I was anxious to see the nature of his charge, and to become acquainted with his flock. I went to inaugurate a course of weekly Advent services. We slept one night there, and a bitter night it was, at the house of General W——, one of his kind and hospitable parishioners : the thermometer was much below zero. I found the congregation small, the place having known better days when it was a military station.

Ten days later, December 11th, I made a tedious railway journey of six hours to Lennoxville, to attend a Corporation meeting at the College.

The Building is handsome and in excellent taste, and it has every advantage which the healthiness and beauty of its position can give. But both the College, and also the School attached to it, have lately been in a depressed state, and much need a revival. The chief reason why the Institution has lost the confidence of Churchmen here, is that it has earned the character (somewhat unjustly perhaps) of nurturing extreme opinions in its students. This however there is at present a great desire to rectify. At the time of my visit the Rector of the school was on the point of leaving, and another has been since appointed, who is likely to give general confidence, and to restore the school to the popularity it certainly deserves.

At the College a good classical education is given, and degrees are conferred. A theological department is also connected with it. But its distance from Montreal is a great disadvantage; and as a Training Institution for our students it is therefore not satisfactory. It is just within the Quebec Diocese, the Bishop and myself being joint visitors.

The next day was given to business; and there was a large party at the Rector's in the evening. On the following morning Dr. N——, the Principal, drove me to Sherbrook, where I attended an important missionary meeting, the Bishop of

Quebec in the chair. The Town-hall was completely full, and the meeting interesting. They received me most kindly; but I fear that many must have been a little disappointed by the tameness and meagreness of my address.

After a very wearying railway journey, the train being constantly impeded by the snow, I reached Montreal six hours after time! The cars are usually heated to a fearful temperature by a stove at either end, and scarcely any escape is allowed for the vitiated air. For this reason I much dislike Canadian railway travelling in winter.

Later in January I passed a Sunday at St. John's, once a garrisoned town, and still a place of some importance, about twenty-five miles from Montreal. My wife accompanied me. St. John's and six other places in the Diocese were constituted rectories by Royal Patent in the reign of George III. They still retain their rank, but enjoy no other advantages arising from their dignified nomenclature, except it be that the nomination of the clergyman is with the parishioners, subject to the approval of the Bishop.

Mr. D——, the rector, greeted us at the station, and had a large party of his parishioners to meet us in the evening. This plan gives one an excellent opportunity of becoming acquainted with the Church people in the different parishes, and they seem much to like it.

We had a wet Sunday, but good congregations both here and also at Christieville, a pretty village over the river, where we went for afternoon Service. At the latter place the church was crowded, many having come from St. John's, where the Service was suspended for the occasion.

Next day, January 24th, we went to Sebrevois, a missionary Institution, ten miles from St. John's. Mr. M,—— drove us in his comfortable sleigh and pair, and Mr. M'G—— and a large party followed. The country is rather low, and had been completely flooded ; the consequence was that the road was one continuous sheet of ice, over which our sleighs glided most joyously. As an evidence of the severity of the weather, I observed, as we went along, that a fringe of ice had formed upon the eyelashes of one of our fair companions.

Sebrevois is supported partly by the Colonial Church Society, and partly by local subscriptions; and has been, and still is, extremely useful. It is in the midst of a French-speaking population ; and consists of a large school, containing about fifty boys and girls, chiefly French Canadians, a few of whom are Roman Catholics. There is also a church which is a rallying point for the few Protestants in the neighbourhood. I subsequently confirmed twenty-eight persons, and was greatly

pleased with the intelligence and Christian spirit
which evidently prevailed there.

We had Morning Service; the Litany being
read in French; the singing half French and half
English; and my sermon, which of course was
English, although understood by most of the audi-
ence, was repeated in French by Mr. L——, at
least the substance of it. We afterwards dined at
the simple parsonage—about twenty of us—and
then returned to St. John's, and home to Montreal,
thanking God for what we had seen and heard.
The expedition had been a satisfactory one, and
we had enjoyed it much.

Early in the following month I had engaged
myself to be at Waterloo, but was forced to put off
my visit by telegram, on account of the inclemency
of the weather, and the drifts of snow which had
blocked up the line of railway.

I started however a few days later, hearing that
the line was clear. The two Mr. L——s met me
on my arrival, and we hastened off to church, for
which I was a little late, in consequence of the
stoppage of the train. There was a capital congregation in a most unecclesiastical-looking building,
which I am happy to say they are soon to vacate
for a handsome Church, which the parishioners are
building at a considerable cost and with much
taste. On my return to the parsonage I found the

house filled with about forty visitors, who had been invited to meet me. There is something very primitive and genial in these gatherings of the church people around their Bishop, and it makes one feel that the Office is appreciated.

The next day was bright and beautiful; but the thermometer was lower than on any day in the winter—nearly thirty degrees *below zero.* It is remarkable how little one feels this excessive cold, so long as there is an absence of wind. The dryness of the air makes it bearable.

In the afternoon we drove to South Stukeley, where we had an Evening Service, to which the people were summoned without much notice. I of course preached according to invariable custom. Indeed, I have done so at every service that I have attended on my tours, with one exception: and I am sometimes almost a marvel to myself, preaching for two or three days successively without any great fatigue. I never could have done this in England; but God has strengthened me for the work He has given me to do. He does indeed fit the back for the burden it has to carry.

Our drive back to Waterloo was very pleasant. It was a thorough Canadian night, the moon and stars wondrously bright, and the snow perfectly clean and white. Mr. A——, the Incumbent, is a good man; but in very weak health, and greatly

needing rest.   He and his wife suffer many privations, chiefly resulting from insufficiency of salary,
and from the difficulty in this country of getting a
servant.   This is no solitary case among the clergy ;
and for their uncomplaining and cheerful acceptance of this state of things one cannot but greatly
admire them.

I returned home by train next morning to
Montreal.   A very early start was needful ; and
my kind hostess, knowing my chilly nature, and
mindful of my comfort, took good care that I
should not leave her roof cold or breakfastless.
Long before dawn I was awakened by a white
figure flitting noiselessly into my room with hot
coals and wood ; and in a few short seconds, before,
as she hoped, I could wake up, she had lighted my
fire and disappeared.   She little knew that, in the
kindness of her heart, she had effectually roused
me, and had thus shortened my night's rest, though
she had certainly won my warmest gratitude.

Two more excursions were made this winter.
One of these was to Mascouche, which is a village about twenty-five miles from Montreal, on
Saturday, February 13th.   This time, also, I had
the comfort of my wife's company.   Mr. G——, the
clergyman of Mascouche, came to fetch us in his
sleigh.   On leaving our house we met the Prince
taking one of his early drives to the Barracks.   It

was always a pleasure to meet him, and he had
a genial word or two to help us on our journey.
We stopped at St. Vincent de Paul on our way,
where we dined, and I held a Confirmation for the
prisoners in the Reformatory. At the time of my
visit, there were 130 in the Prison, a small minority
of whom were Protestants, under the care of Mr.
A——, the Chaplain. I inspected the building
with the Warden, who kindly lionized me over it,
and showed me great civility. The convicts were
ranged in the yard for our review, and I was much
struck with their appearance, for crime had sadly
left its stamp on most of their countenances. Six
were presented for Confirmation. I spoke kindly
to them, and felt much for them, knowing that if
any of them were at all impressed for good they
would indeed stand a poor chance among such
companions.

We had about twelve miles on to Mascouche,
over a bleak country with snow and high wind in
our faces. However, we arrived safe and sound at
Mr. G——'s parsonage, where a little party met us,
consisting of the Squire of the place, Mr. P——, and
his wife, and Mr. and Mrs. B——, who had lately
come from England, and established themselves
there.

The next day was Sunday, and a bright, clear,
cold day it was, the snow lying thick and crisp upon
the ground. We had a nice Morning Service, and

in the Afternoon we went to Terrebonne church, a simple wooden building six miles off.

On Monday we had planned a longish expedition, to visit the Missions of New Glasgow, twelve miles off, and Kilkenny eight miles beyond. A fall of snow however alarmed the ladies, and they stayed behind. Mr. P—— drove us in his tandem sleigh, and a most severe drive we had; so much so, that we were forced to abandon all thoughts of getting beyond New Glasgow. We had service there, and I preached as well as I was able, my teeth chattering with cold. The church is dreary and barn-like, and the Mission in rather a broken and forlorn condition. After dining at Mr. G——'s, one of the Churchwardens, we again mounted our sleighs. The snow was deep, and the road but indistinctly marked, so that for a great part of the way we were forced to travel at a foot's pace.

On the whole, it was the roughest and most trying expedition that I have made. The scene was very striking, with a sheet of snow on all sides; and the sleigh and our fur robes made it thoroughly Canadian. The fact however of the Bishop driving up to the church-door in a tandem, was thought nothing of in this land of sleighs, and snow, and necessities. Had it not been for my admirable fur coat and cap, the gifts of my dear Sisters in England, also a thick cape and a capuchin hood over all, with my wife's 'Cloud' closely covering

my face, and acting as a respirator, I could not
have borne the cold. The skill too of our charioteer
made me feel quite safe.

We dined that evening with Mr. P——, who
sent his *Traineau* to fetch us, and to take us back
to the parsonage. These traineaux, which are in-
tended only to carry wood, are capital rustic
conveyances for a party. They are capable of
holding almost an unlimited number; there are
no seats, all being obliged to stand, and hold on as
best they can. We much enjoyed our short drive,
as the night was beautiful and the weather warmer.
Mr. P—— drove us the next day in his comfortable
sleigh, with good horses, to Montreal. Mr. G——
and Mr. and Mrs. B—— accompanying us as far
as Terrebonne.

My last winter Visitation of any importance was
a four days' tour, on which I started by train at
seven o'clock on Saturday, March 5th. I left home
with rather a heavy heart; but the day was bright
and fine. Mr. S——, a layman, met me at the
station, and went with me as far as St. Hyacinthe,
where we had a Missionary Meeting, he and I being
the only speakers. He then left me; and I went on
by train to Acton, where I slept at Mr. W——'s
parsonage. Mr. H——, a farmer, from Boscobel,
had come to meet me, according to his kind promise, and to convey me next morning to the

Mission in which he is interested, consisting of
Boscobel, North Ely, and Roxton Falls. This
Mission was at the time without a pastor, and
he had urged me so strongly to visit it, that I
could not refuse, though I rather dreaded the
journey.

Early on Sunday morning, Mr. H—— was at
the door with his sleigh, and we drove together to
North Ely, a bad road, through a rough and only
partially cleared country. He had two little Canadian horses. These are most serviceable animals,
and just suited to the rough roads and inclement
weather; they are very active, sure-footed, and
endurant, and will stand being tied up in any cold
place, according to the custom of the country.
They are about fourteen hands high, and rather
ungainly in their appearance, with narrow chests;
but they trot away at a famous pace, and are very
handy and understanding, being treated quite as
friends of the family. The harness is usually of
rather an uncared-for type, but light and useful.
Mr. W——, the Acton clergyman, most kindly
followed in his sleigh, in order to assist me in the
service.

After a pretty good jolting along a road of fourteen miles, we suddenly turned a corner in the
midst of the Bush, and came upon a most picturesque scene. There was the humble school-
house in which our service was to be held, with

about twenty sleighs and horses all round it, and the greater part of the congregation assembled at the door in their buffalo coats and furs, ready for the Service. Some of the horses were tied to posts or trees, and some perfectly loose, but standing most quietly until they were required. It snowed a little, but the day was not cold. Our horses shared with the rest, being tied up without the slightest shelter, after their three hours' drive. The whole scene outside the school-house had the appearance of a fair.

On entering the room I found a scorching stove, and the temperature up to about 70°; and as there were double windows, and no aperture for the ingress of fresh air, and the place was crammed full, I began to fear lest we should be stifled. So, after making a few signals of distress, I got them to open the door and give our lungs a chance. The good people had decorated the school with fir-boughs and strips of coloured paper, so that it had the appearance of a series of German trees. Mr. W——, who knew the congregation to be a motley one, made up of all denominations, wisely brought with him a number of Prayer-books, and gave out the page when he passed from one prayer to another. Thus we had a nice, simple, earnest service ; and I preached from St. John, iii. 3, cheering them with the assurance that I would do my best to find them a clergyman, which I

E

have since done. I humbly hope that God may have blest my words.

Mr. W—— then left me for his own Evening Service; and Mr. H—— drove me on to his home, eight miles off, where we dined. In the evening we had another Service at Boscobel, Mr. L——, from Waterloo, having at some inconvenience come over to help us. Mr. O——, a lay-Reader and a good man, was for the time in charge of the Mission.

My host drove me next morning back to Acton, a distance of twelve miles; and from thence I went to Upton, and on to Lennoxville on College business.

My visit to Ely and Boscobel was very satisfactory, as it gave me an insight into one of our roughest Missions, and the people had expressed a great wish to have me among them. Mr. H——, at whose house I slept, is a well-to-do farmer, who came out to Canada some thirty years ago. By his shrewdness and energy he has risen in the world, and has now a nice house and a considerable property, living in quite a patriarchal manner with his children and grandchildren all gathered around him. To each of his sons he has given a piece of land, which they work themselves. He has also living under his roof a faithful old servant, who has been with him twenty years, and is content to labour on with his master, although he has saved enough to make himself independent. When in England he had been a travelling musician, and had given way to intemperance ; but during the twenty years of his Canadian life he has been a sober and respectable man, as well as a most faithful helper to his master.

On the morning of my departure from Mr. H——'s we breakfasted at seven ; and the mother and three sons appeared in their ordinary working dress. The father had specially desired this, he told me ; for though he wished to do honour to his guest, he wanted to show me how they lived, and that work was the rule with all.

I was glad, as I always am, to reach home, and specially glad to have accomplished such a feat as a winter visit to Ely and Boscobel, and felt myself none the worse for all the bumping, and jolting, and other experiences to which I had been subject.

CHAPTER VI.

A WINTER IN MONTREAL.

I HARDLY know a pleasanter place in which to pass the winter months than Montreal. Its cheerfulness, and at the same time its quietness—for, instead of the rumbling of carriages along the streets, they glide noiselessly over the snow—its many appliances to keep out the cold—the kindness of its inhabitants—the facilities for moving about, &c.—all make it a charming place of residence in the winter. We were living in a most comfortable and convenient house in Drummond Street, which had been provided for us by some generous members of our Church; and here the time passed as happily as it could in the absence of those beloved ones whose companionship we sorely missed. I had now a good deal of quiet time for gathering up the arrears of work, which a year without a Bishop had accumulated in the Diocese, and also of becoming acquainted with the clergy and congregations in the city of Montreal.

There are nine churches in the town : most of them in a prosperous condition; and certainly the staff of clergy is above the ordinary standard both in point of earnestness and power. My interest was of course in the Cathedral primarily ; but the other churches also had a strong claim upon me. In the former I held my first Ordination, consisting of three persons, who were admitted to the Order of Deacons. This was a very solemn time ; but the actual ceremony was in a measure spoilt by the peculiar inconvenience of the structure for such a Service ; so much so, that I felt it would be better to hold the three following Ordinations in other churches.

As I found a deficiency of labourers in the Diocese, I was thankful for this accession of three promising men to our ranks. My present desire is rather to raise than to lower the standard of ministerial acquirements, feeling that the greatness of the work and the advance of education demand it.

The congregations in our city Churches are generally good, and the services well ordered. There is a Sunday-school attached to each church; and some of these are excellently managed and numerously attended. At the two largest the numbers amount to five and six hundred. These schools are in some instances held in the basements of the churches, in a large room almost underground. They are attended by all classes, even the highest, and the number of teachers is large. On one day in the winter all these Sunday-schools

assembled in St. George's Church, and I preached
to them.   The Service was especially interesting ;
and my feeling was that I had seldom addressed a
more important congregation.

There is also an abundance of Charitable Institutions at Montreal — Hospitals, Church Homes,
Friendly Societies, &c., and all well managed.   St.
George's society, St. Andrew's, and St. Patrick's,
lay themselves out to receive poor emigrants on
their arrival in Canada ; also to be generally useful
to their countrymen, and to keep up a national
feeling amongst them.

I have scarcely ever seen a beggar in the streets
of Montreal, or in the country.   There is a great
absence of poverty, except perhaps among the
lowest French population.   Of course, there are no
Poor-Laws or Unions here ; but there are several
charitable Refuges, in which the needy and friend-
less are cared for.   And among the Roman Catholics especially there are many Institutions on an
enormous scale.

Besides the several fine churches belonging to
our own Communion, which would be an ornament
to any town, there are handsome buildings
belonging to other denominations.   Between the
various sections of the Protestant Church there
exists a friendly rivalry, but an absence of that
bitterness which sometimes disgraces the members
of differing religious bodies.   We, who are Church-

men, are decided Churchmen, perhaps even more so
than in England; but we honour the feelings of
those who conscientiously differ from us, though
we are persuaded that they would be great gainers
by joining our ranks; and earnestly long for the
time when 'there shall be one Lord, and His
name one.'

The Roman Catholics are by far the most
numerous body, and have some fine churches,
though not strictly in harmony with our English
tastes. Happily there is at present a kindly
feeling between the Roman Catholics and Protestants, each pursuing their own course without
molesting the other. And it is well that it should
be so, for little would indeed be gained on either
side if controversy and contention were the order
of the day. As a Reformed Church, we desire, by
God's help, to hold our own, and 'contend earnestly for the faith once delivered to the saints.'
But we wish at the same time to speak the truth
in love, carefully avoiding all bitterness and harsh-
ness of language, which only wounds without
healing.

But now—to speak more generally of the state
of things at Montreal—the whole city is at this
season in its winter's dress. The roofs of the
houses, and also the streets, are covered with
snow from the beginning of December to the end

of April—five long months.   In the majority of
the streets, no attempt is made to remove it from
the wooden side-walks; but it becomes beaten
down, and makes a solid footpath.   Sometimes the
walking is very bad, and almost dangerous, so
that elderly gentlemen, like myself, are glad to
put on 'creepers,' which are something like the
spikes which are attached to cricket shoes, or to
the 'crampons,' which are used in Switzerland
for crossing the glaciers.   However, the people at
Montreal are not much given to walking; and
last winter Mrs. Oxenden and myself were about
the most persevering pedestrians in the place:
and this, I am sure, contributed not a little to
our health.

The sleighs, darting about from street to street,
are most picturesque.   Some of them are very
handsomely got up, with an abundance of furs and
other trappings.   The motion is most agreeable,
and the pace delightful; and even in the keenest
weather, provided there is a tolerable absence of
wind, one suffers little from cold.   A fur coat, and
cap with ear-pads, completely protect one.   We
have sometimes been out at night in an open
sleigh, when the thermometer has been consider-
ably below zero, without feeling it so much as an
ordinary cold night in England.   They usually
hold four persons, and being almost on the ground,
and most of them without doors, one steps in and

out with the greatest ease. The hired sleighs, of which there are plenty, are clean and good, and the owners take a pride in the robes with which they are provided. Most people keep a sleigh of their own ; but we were an exception, and found but little inconvenience. One has occasionally to satisfy oneself that one's nose and ears are all right, as they are sometimes frozen before the possessor is at all aware of his condition. Ordinary precautions however are sufficient to prevent such a catastrophe.

The roofs of the houses and the Church-spires are often of zinc, and their appearance is very dazzling and pretty. But in the country wooden shingles are generally used, and are very serviceable, lasting about five-and-twenty years, and keeping out the wet and cold extremely well. Few objects are more striking than a country church with a zinc spire glittering in the noon-day sun.

I know not how it is, but there are more conflagrations in Canada than elsewhere. A fire at Montreal is a thing of weekly occurrence, and even more so at Quebec. There is an admirable Fire Brigade ; and the whole system is perfect in its arrangements. There are telegraphic wires, which communicate between all parts of the town and the engine-stations, and the supply of water is excellent. The plan of operations is this : when a fire breaks out, some one immediately runs to the nearest telegraphic box, of which there are more than one in each street, and having procured the key which is known to be deposited in an adjoining house, the box is opened, and a little button presents itself, which, being pulled, conveys the alarm, by means of the telegraphic wire, to the Engine-house. There the horses are kept harnessed, and a body of men are always in readiness, so that in the course of a few minutes the engine is at the door of the house in danger. In the country, large tracts of woodland are sometimes on fire for days together, and it is very difficult to extinguish them; but of this I shall speak further in another chapter.

I have said that Prince Arthur was in Montreal during this winter. His Royal Highness might be seen day after day driving his phaeton and pair down to the Barracks after an early breakfast, or walking home a couple of miles in the afternoon. There was no parade about his movements, but all was natural, and yet most correct and princelike. His presence among us added not a little to the enjoyment of all. Twice he honoured us by being present at an evening reception at our house, which enabled us to entertain all our kind friends, to the number of some hundreds, who had given us so cordial and hearty a welcome. The Prince shone much on such occasions, being full of kindness, and showing always that good breeding for which England is remarkable.

The Skating Rink is a great winter feature in this city, and to this the Prince paid almost a daily visit. It is a very large and handsome building, the flooring of which is a smooth sheet of ice, constantly renewed by the inlet of a flood of water. Here hundreds of persons may be seen skating every day, and especially in the afternoon, among whom are some of the best skaters in the world, of both sexes.

We went there on one grand occasion, when every skater wore a fancy costume. It was one of the most beautiful sights I ever beheld. The place was hung with the gayest flags, most tastefully arranged : it was splendidly lighted, and filled with skaters in their fancy dresses, and lookers-on. The Prince invited us, and also the Bishop of Quebec and Mrs. Williams, who were with us at the time, to his gallery, from whence we had a delightful bird's-eye view of all that was going on. It was indeed a fairy scene to look upon. The skating was wonderful, and the dresses gorgeous. On this occasion the Prince was only a spectator.

The great St. Lawrence is of course, frozen over during the winter; but the state of the ice is totally different to that which we had pictured to ourselves. I expected to see a smooth, even sheet of ice, spread over the bed of the river, so that upon this even surface people could walk and drive *ad libitum:* but no such thing; the river is covered with an irregular mass of snow and ice jammed together upon the water, and presenting all kinds of shapes. In this state of chaos, it is perfectly impassable, until two or three roads are made upon it leading to villages on the other side. Along these roads there is a considerable traffic, as provisions, and especially hay, are continually being brought in from the country. A few places are cleared for skating, but these are very few and but little used. The whole appearance resembles an irregular glacier more than anything else.

Before leaving England, I was charged by my doctor to ride ; and I was one of the few who steadily persevered in this exercise during the whole winter. It was a great refreshment to me, when wearied with indoor work, to get an hour on horseback before luncheon. There were but few days when I was prevented by the cold, although I confess that I had sometimes a difficulty in keeping up a sufficient amount of circulation. For this exercise, which contributed not a little to my health, I was indebted to a kind officer commanding the Artillery, Colonel G——, who pretended that I did him much service by keeping his two horses in exercise.

The custom of paying friendly visits on New Year's Day has long prevailed among the upper classes, both of French and English, in Canada.

These visits are paid by gentlemen only, the ladies remaining at home to receive visitors. An exception is kindly made in the case of the Bishop and the Clergy, who are allowed to consider themselves as the visited on this occasion. We received on New Year's Day nearly 300 visits, and among them we were honoured by a special visit from the Prince.

It is a genial and time-honoured custom, and one that I should be very sorry to see discontinued. It draws out much kind feeling; and I have known cases where it has been the signal for a reconciliation between persons who have been long estranged from each other.

Dinner-parties are frequent in Montreal. There is perhaps a little too much expense devoted to them; and this prevents all but the wealthy from indulging in such hospitalities.

I should say that the general cost of living here is much the same as in an ordinary English town. House-rent is high, and so are all kinds of grocery and dress; whereas meat, poultry, fish, &c. are reasonable and excellent. The meat is fairly good, but not perhaps first-rate. The beef is somewhat hard, and the mutton is generally too young, being usually little more than grown-up lamb. There are no butchers' shops in the streets, but every kind of meat is to be had in the public markets, which are held daily, and are admirably supplied. It is by no means unusual to see the greatest Ladies sallying forth after breakfast to make their purchases. Much of the meat is killed in December and kept frozen through the winter; but in this state it loses somewhat of its freshness and flavour. It is not at all uncommon in passing one of the markets, or when driving into the country, to see a large hog standing stiff on all fours, looking quite alive, but having ceased to breathe for many weeks.

The turkeys and fowls are remarkably cheap and abundant; and the game, which consists of partridges, prairie-hens (a kind of grouse), quails, snow-birds, &c., are excellent. One often sees a string of cock-pheasants hanging up outside a grocer's shop, which have been sent over from Blenheim or Stowe; also English hares, of which there is only a very debased mongrel kind to be met with in this country.

The Canadians are somewhat demonstrative in their sorrows. The funeral cavalcades are of enormous dimensions. It is a common thing to see a hearse followed by forty or fifty carriages, and sometimes by one or two hundred mourners. There is a very picturesque and beautiful Protestant Cemetery on the north side of the mountain, about three miles from the town; and here most of the burials take place. There is however something very sad and unsatisfactory about the ceremony,

for, owing to the severe cold, there is usually no
service in the open air, as in England; and from
the impenetrable state of the ground, no interment
can take place in winter, but the body is consigned
for a time to a public vault within the enclosure
of the cemetery. The service therefore is read in
the church before leaving the town.

Montreal is decidedly a healthy city during the
winter, and unhealthy in the summer, especially
for children. There is no lack of medical advice,
and that of a high character. As to the legal
profession, there are almost as many lawyers as
there are clients; and yet I am sure that the
Canadians are not a quarrelsome or combative
people.

But I must now be bringing my chapter to a
close, and the winter too. Suddenly, in the end
of April, the thermometer mounted up from zero
to forty degrees. Two or three days of hot
weather came, and then a soaking rain. The
sleighs were suddenly put by, and wheels once
more were the order of the day. The snow and
ice disappear in wondrously quick time, almost
before one is able to put by one's furs, and take
to a more seasonable dress. The transition from
winter to summer is remarkable: there is scarcely
any intervening spring.

On the first of May half the people of Montreal change their houses. For about three days

huge waggons piled up with furniture are to be
seen in every street, and innumerable auctions take
place. We, among the rest, moved to a fresh
house, which we have taken for a year, when we
hope to get into our new and permanent abode,
to which I have ventured to give the name of
' Bishop's Court,' there to remain fixed so long
as God shall be pleased to keep us here.

CHAPTER VII.

A SUMMER IN THE EASTERN TOWNSHIPS.

MONTREAL, as I have already said, is not desirable as a place of residence in the summer; for, although the upper parts of the city are airy and pleasant, it is, for some reason which I cannot fathom, certainly not healthy, especially for children, during the hot weather. I suppose there is something defective in the drainage of the town, although I certainly should not have come to this conclusion, had it not so frequently been pressed upon me.

After casting about for a place of retreat, we fixed upon the little village of Dunham, in the Eastern Townships, about fifty miles south of Montreal. Most people choose gayer and more fashionable quarters, where they may get sea-air; such as Portland, a sea-port in the States, or Murray Bay, Riviére du Loup, or Cacouna at the entrance of the Gulf below Quebec. Others again are content with Lachine, a village near the junction of the St. Lawrence and Ottawa, which unite a little higher up, and here present a noble expanse of water. This is a nice change for those who like

F

boating, and wish to be near Montreal; but the
place is not otherwise very attractive.

We decided upon a pretty little new house in
the peaceful village of Dunham, because we longed
for perfect quietude after the publicity of a winter
at Montreal; also because it lay in the very heart
of the Diocese, and I was anxious to become better
acquainted with my clergy and their people.   It
also gave me a favourable opportunity of holding
several Confirmations, with scarcely the necessity
of spending a single night from home.

Here we arrived at the end of June, immediately after the Synod and its anxieties were fairly
over.   And never did I seem to breathe more
freely than when I found myself with my wife,
child, and servants, established in our village
home.

A large tract of country to the south of the St.
Lawrence goes by the name of the Eastern Townships.   In the reign of George III. the Government
laid out this part of the country in plots of land,
each comprising ten or twelve square miles, and
called a township, having its own separate munici-
pality.   These townships extend from Bedford and
Stanbridge in the west to some distance beyond
Richmond in the east, and on the south they touch
the line or border of the States.   The larger portion of this tract is in the Diocese of Montreal:
the rest in Quebec.   The country has a more

riant and flourishing appearance than other parts of Lower Canada. It is tolerably cleared, and is pretty well cultivated. And if it were not for the long and severe winters, I should say it must be as fine a spot for farming enterprise as any in the world.

The whole country, from Philipsburg on the Missisquoi Bay eastward towards Memphre Magog, and from thence to Brome Lake, and across to Waterloo, Shefford, Iron Hill, and Sweetsburg, is extremely pretty. In many respects it reminded us of parts of Switzerland. The mountains are low, but beautifully wooded, and of mountain-like formation. There is a little lack of water in the district, with the exception of two or three beautiful lakes; and the wooden buildings certainly cannot compare with the picturesque Swiss châlets. The country is studded about with innumerable barns and outhouses; but they lack the projecting eaves, the carved work, and, more than all, the colouring of the same class of buildings in Switzerland. Still it is a beautiful country, and we were charmed with many of our drives.

My first step was to buy a little horse and carriage, as I found it was almost impossible to hire. The usual conveyances in these parts are called waggons or buggies. They are extremely light, on four very slight wheels, and holding two persons. The wheels are very high and near together, and

the whole carriage weighs less than an English
pony-carriage. They are neat enough in themselves, but they are usually unwashed, and therefore have a slovenly appearance, and the harness
is not of the best, nor is there much blacking
bestowed upon it. Every one has his carriage here,
as no one walks. If a person comes round with
wild raspberries, she calls in her buggy ; and as
for walking a mile, it is a thing unheard of; every
one drives.

I was told of a beggar in an adjoining parish,
who keeps his carriage, and drives from house to
house collecting alms. So we, like our neighbours,
fell into the Dunham way, and drove about the
country, almost forgetting that we had legs to walk
with.

It is curious to see the number of carriages that
are gathered around the churches. Close to every
Church, there is commonly a large half-open shed ;
and this affords shelter to the waggons in the summer, and the sleighs in the winter, the horses
patiently remaining during service.

The roads are mostly unstoned, but they are
fairly good, are most pleasant to drive upon,
and I am not sure that I would exchange them
for a hard English flint road. At all events we
were quite content with them.

There seemed at first to be one great deficiency
in our Dunham house. There was no garden

attached to it, and no vegetables were to be bought in the place. But our wants were abundantly supplied, and at times even superabundantly, by the kindness of our neighbours, who sent us far more beautiful vegetables of all kinds than we could have got at Montreal. Potatoes, cabbages, peas, French beans, tomatoes, Indian corn, cauliflowers. melons, &c., found their way into our kitchen, and were all the sweeter for being free-will gifts. One farmer, a stranger, drove over from a village, twelve miles off, with a beautiful specimen of his garden produce as an offering to the Bishop. The Indian corn is eaten in a semi-ripe state as a vegetable. There are various ways of serving it; but I think the best, though perhaps not the most elegant, is to boil the whole upon the cone. You then spread a little butter upon it, and eat it *au naturel;* and it is really very good.

Both the wild and cultivated Flowers are inferior to those in England. The latter grow too luxuriantly; and it is rare to meet with a really trim flower-garden.

There are but few Birds that make their home in Canada. Most of those which are to be seen in summer are birds of passage. Of these some are very pretty, though, as songsters, they are inferior to those we have in England. The prettiest bird is perhaps the so-called canary. In shape it is almost like a sparrow, but it is

strikingly handsome—a deep yellow, with very
defined patches of greenish brown. The colours
are more decided than those of the tame canaries
which are seen in England. One constantly sees
them in companies of half-a-dozen by the road-
side ; and they are so tame that one would expect
them to be content with a prison life ; but this is
not so, and one rarely sees them in cages.

The Canadian robin is as unlike our English
redbreast as possible. It much more resembles
the thrush. I at first fancied that we had not left
all our friends the rooks behind us ; but, upon
closer inspection, I found that my black acquaint-
ances were something between a carrion crow and
a rook. They have however a very homelike look,
and a familiar caw, which reminds us of rookeries
in the dear old land.

The little humming-bird is rather rare, and
they are seldom seen but in flower-gardens. They
are more like butterflies or gadflies than birds,
both as regards their size and their habits. There
is, I believe, but one species commonly met with,
but that is very beautiful. It seems almost
unaccountable that this very delicate little creature
should take so long a flight to visit us for merely
a month or two in the height of the summer.

There are but few snakes in this country, and
none, I believe, of venomous character. There
is a slim kind of squirrel, which is very domestic,

and seems to delight in exhibiting its antics in public. And there is also a little fellow between a squirrel and a rat, called a chipmink, which is beautifully mottled.

The farmers around Dunham are many of them substantial men; their fathers and grand-fathers having settled here and purchased land, clearing it by degrees. As there is a great deficiency of labourers, they are obliged to do a great deal themselves; and certainly many of them are singularly active, busy, hard-working men. In this immediate neighbourhood a great deal of very excellent cheese is made, and every person has his staff of cows, varying from twenty to fifty. These are milked by the road-side, morning and evening; the milk is deposited in zinc pails, and placed on a platform, and a cart comes trotting by, picks up the various contributions, and carries them to the nearest cheese-factory, where each lot is weighed and duly accounted for. Some of these factories receive the milk of a thousand cows. The cheeses, which usually weigh about sixty or seventy pounds, are sent either into the States or to England, and better I have never tasted.

Soon after our arrival the hay-making season began. This is a stirring time. The grass is mostly mown by machinery, and it is often cut, made, and carried on the same day! Indeed, from its ripeness, and the dryness of the atmosphere, it needs scarcely any making, but is fit to carry almost as soon as it is mown down. It is then deposited in barns, a stack being a rare sight in these parts.

The corn-harvest follows almost immediately. The most productive crop is the Indian corn, which this year was very fine, and was a good month earlier than usual. A few hop-gardens are to be seen here and there; but they are not cultivated in the Kentish style. My dear old Pluckley Parishioners would cast a very contemptuous eye upon them. And yet in spite of weeds and very scanty manuring, they produce a fair crop, and I have no doubt that, if more expense and labour were bestowed upon them, they would grow well, and make a profitable return.

The mode of farming is very different from that which I have been used to. Much is done by machinery, and little by manual labour. What strikes one perhaps most is the speed with which both men and horses move here. Instead of a huge Kentish plough drawn by four fat horses, you see a light instrument with a couple of quick ponies, which the driver, with the reins round his wrist, steers most dexterously between the roots and rocks, with which the fields abound. Then they carry their loads in very light waggons, the driver perched on the top, and driving with reins at a

good brisk trot. Thus they whisk up their produce
and carry it off to the barn, whilst our labourers
would be crawling about the field, and deliberating
as to their next step.

We were much amused one day to watch this
process, as we were taking a drive along the high
road. We saw, in an adjoining corn-field, a waggon pretty well loaded, and coming towards us.
We discovered the only gap in the fence whereby
it could properly make its exit, and that rather a
steep and perilous one. So we stopped to see how
the waggon would fare. It came up swaying
terribly from side to side, the driver standing on
the top with his legs very far apart, not only keeping his own balance, but poising the whole load by
the nice adjustment of his own weight. When he
arrived at the gap he paused, as if to take aim, and
then, giving a shout of encouragement to his horses,
he dashed through, and making a sharp turn into
the road, trotted along to the barn, and deposited
his oats there in perfect safety. It was a great feat
of dexterity, and would have astonished not a
little our English waggoners if they could have
seen it.

It strikes me that, considering the great scarcity
of labour, most of the farmers have too large a
tract under cultivation. The consequence is that the
land is insufficiently worked, and not made to yield
half that it is capable of producing. There is more

to be done than the few industrious hands can properly accomplish.

A great number of English emigrants came out this summer. But most of them were disposed to pass on to Upper Canada, rather than seek their fortunes here. There is however a good living to be got, and a fair prospect for the future, for a settler in the Eastern Townships. What is chiefly wanted is willingness to work, and steadiness of character.

Two emigrants were brought specially under my notice, who had both come from my neighbourhood in Kent. One was a sturdy, sensible, sober, well-educated man, who was fit to be a foreman or bailiff on an English farm. He had left his wife and children behind, and, poor fellow, he longed to send for them, but the means were wanting. However he scraped together enough to nearly pay their passage. This is the stamp of man that is wanted; and if he perseveres, and is content to work as a farm-labourer for a few years, he will soon be likely to save enough to buy a little land, and thrive in this country.

The other was the son of a clergyman in an adjoining parish to Pluckley. His father could not afford to start him with any capital; but he desired to emigrate; and being young and strong he determined to try his fortune in Canada. So he took his passage for Liverpool as a common emigrant.

The day after his arrival in Montreal, we met him in the street on his way to our house. He was looking pretty well, but he had suffered not a little from his voyage. He had roughed it, he said, before; but never had he passed through such an ordeal as his emigrant's passage. He was one of four hundred, who were closely packed in one of the regular Line Packets. He had paid the regulation price, six pounds, and was treated after the regulation fashion.

After being a few days with us, he regained his spirits, and cast about for employment. He soon engaged himself to a wealthy farmer, and there he set to with all his heart, turning his hand to anything required of him, and there he remained till after the following harvest. Had he been enabled to remain in the country, I doubt not he would have succeeded; but a death in his family, I grieve to say, called him home.

There are numbers of schools in and around Dunham; about one, I believe, to every square mile. Indeed, there is no lack of schools in Canada generally. Many of these however are very small, and the instruction is defective. There is a peculiarly desolate and unpicturesque appearance about them; and certainly, if the charms of education are represented by the buildings, there is little to attract. There is also this great and radical fault—the education is secular and religionless; and consequently that which ought to be a blessing to this infant country, will, I fear, prove to be its curse. Private efforts should be made to remedy this evil. A few good church schools, where religion is the recognised basis, and a Christian tone cultivated, would be an inestimable boon to Canada.

In the first part of our stay, I was chiefly engaged with my Confirmations, which I held in most of the parishes of the Deanery. The number of candidates generally averaged about fifteen. They were always well conducted, and generally seemed to be impressed with the solemnity of the rite. It gave me an opportunity of gathering the parishioners together, and holding services which the people generally seemed to appreciate, as well as those more immediately concerned; and for these services, I have reason to feel thankful. It is not unusual in a Canadian confirmation to have a large proportion of adults, and even persons of advanced age, among the candidates. I have confirmed an old man of ninety, and several above seventy. Many of these had remained long unbaptized, and have only recently been received into the Church.

During the latter part of my stay in the Townships, I had hoped to be free from work. But this I could not quite manage, as little calls for labour were for ever presenting themselves. A Church had to be opened here, and a special Confirmation to be held there. But still I had a good deal of quiet time to myself, which I greatly enjoyed. And as for ever being quite at liberty, I suppose a Bishop can never expect that; for whether in or out of his Diocese, there are always letters to be written, and matters to be settled, requiring anxious and painful thought. This however is necessarily a characteristic of my work; but I willingly accept it, and am very thankful that my labours are often greatly lightened by the thoughtful consideration of those over whom I am placed.

CHAPTER VIII.

CLOSE OF THE SUMMER.

I FELT a little sad when our short summer drew
to a close We were led to think that the heat
would be intolerable, but we have found it otherwise. The temperature may be higher, but the
heat is less oppressive, than during many a hot
season which I remember in Kent.

We had our little gaieties at Dunham—our
drives, our calls, our sewing-society meetings, and
our tea-parties. These latter are usually the meal of
hospitality. Guests arrive about six, and the little
parlour is well filled. Then, presently, the folding-
doors are thrown open, and a well-spread table
presents itself. There is no stint of provisions.
There are plates of bread cut in the thinnest slices,
cakes of various shapes, and of invariable goodness,
and a profusion of jam, which is served to each
person in a pretty little glass saucer; besides this,
there is plenty of good butter, and sometimes
cheese. Certainly, there is no fear of one's going
home hungry, or of not meeting with a warm
reception. The tea which is most used is from

Japan; it has very much the flavour of our green tea, which is considered so unwholesome in England. This however seems to be perfectly innocuous, and to my palate it is very agreeable. One of the clergy told me that a servant of his, observing that her master preferred black tea and her mistress green, whispered to him confidentially one morning, that she had put some green tea at the bottom of the teapot, and a spoonful or two of black at the top; and that if he would pour his out first, he would get all the black, not calculating that the process of admixture would take place, and render her care for her master's interests somewhat futile.

After tea there is a little friendly talk, and then the pleasant evening generally closes as it ought, with a chapter of the Bible and Prayer. Such at least was usually the case at Dunham, when I have been present.

One of our few great excursions was up the Pinnacle, a little strikingly shaped conical mountain, about seven miles from Dunham, closely wooded almost to the summit, with a bare rocky peak. It was seen from all parts, and appeared to be constantly saying to us, 'Come up, and see what I have to show you.' And as we heard that the ascent was quite worth the pains, we determined that it should tempt us no longer.

So we started one afternoon, and drove to the

foot of the mountain; and our clergyman, Mr.
G——, and his wife, accompanied us. Having had
some experience on the Swiss mountains, though in
a very small way, I of course thought and spoke
somewhat contemptuously of such a trifling walk
as this; but it proved to be a harder afternoon's
work than I had bargained for.

Arrived at the base, we tied up our horses at a
farm; but hearing that the ascent was a case of
impossibility for the ladies, we posted them on a
pleasant woodland slope, from whence they could
see us on reaching the top, and having obtained
some directions from the farmers, we plunged
boldly into the bush. Certainly there was a blind
path, but we were constantly losing it on account
of the number of huge trees, which had been toppled
over by a severe hurricane in the previous week.
However, by mounting continually upwards, we at
length saw the wished-for rock, which we immediately recognised as the goal towards which we
were pressing.

We were quite repaid for our walk, and a
sharp one it certainly was; and though the atmosphere was hazy, we still had a good near view, and
imagined what was beyond.

And now for our descent, which we pictured
to ourselves as a mere bagatelle, and easily to be
accomplished. Well, we began at a merry pace,
but soon lost our bearing. I thought we were

pointing too much to the left; my companion was sure that we were going right. Both proved to be wrong, and I the more so of the two. For when, after a while, we saw daylight again, and emerged from the bush, we found ourselves a good three miles north of the spot from which we had ascended! Hot and tired as we were, we had to press on to reach our party, who, we knew, must be beginning to feel alarmed, as the shadows of evening were gathering around us. And truly they *were* a little alarmed. Finding that we did not arrive, they had gone to the farm; and there the good, kind people fully entered into their anxiety, although they assured them that we had only shared the fate of most travellers, and missed our way, and would soon turn up. One of them however most kindly volunteered to sally forth with his horn in search of us; and two labouring men said that they would also be on the look-out. But presently our welcome arrival set all right; and going into the farm-house, we rested ourselves for half-an-hour, revelled in some new milk, and started home by moonlight.

But our troubles were not over. Mr. and Mrs. G—— led the way in their buggy, and we followed in ours. Our little mare was unusually fresh and impatient, and the harness was evidently not right. I got out and adjusted it; but she did not seem very placid even then. And presently, when going

G

down a steep hill, with a ditch on either side, she fairly jibbed, at one moment refusing to move, and the next darting forward as if she was shot out of a gun, so that I could scarcely hold her. At length, when half way down the hill, she peremptorily refused to go on, and finally backed us into the ditch, locking the fore-wheels across the road. At this critical moment to jump out was our best chance ; and this we did safely with the reins in hand. And then, with the assistance of our kind and active friend, Mr. G——, who had come back in search of us, we coaxed our steed on, and eventually restored her to a better temper.

We did not reach home till ten o'clock ; and there we found our servants gathered on the gallery, having become a little anxious as to what had happened to us. This then was one of our Dunham gaieties, an excursion which I should much like to repeat under other circumstances. And this too was one of the many instances in which God has watched over us, and kept us from harm.

The weather was delightful during our three months' stay at Dunham. The summer was more than ordinarily hot ; but we were never really oppressed by the heat. Certainly, a healthier residence we could not have found.

For about a week the atmosphere was more or less charged with smoke, owing to the burnings in the woods. These fires are sometimes most disastrous. They were unusually so this summer, in consequence of the excessive dryness of the ground. I was told that on one occasion, during a hurricane, the fire travelled over thirty miles of country within an hour—such was the fearful rapidity of its giant strides. Cases occurred too of parents pouring water over their children, in the hope of sheltering them from the burning heat, until at length they were forced to yield them up to the devouring element.

In the neighbourhood of Ottawa, houses, barns, and even villages, were destroyed by the flames. In one of these villages I was to have held a Confirmation, but I was unable to do so, as the people were obliged to watch their homesteads for days and nights together, and much property around them had been utterly destroyed.

The commander of the Fire Brigade writes thus :—

' I encountered sights that for misery and desolation exceeded all I had ever previously experienced. Towards Bell's Corner, for miles, not a habitation was to be found. At one place I observed a man sitting on a charred pine-log, with flannel shirt, and no hat or covering for his head : his story was short ; " A few hours ago," he said, pointing to the smouldering embers, " there stood three barns, two of them filled with grain ; there stood the cow-shed, and there the stables ; now you can see the carcases of eight cows, forty sheep, and nine hogs." Then, turning round, and pointing across the road, he said, " There stood our home, now all is gone, the fruits of thirty years' hard labour. In yonder swamp are my wife and bairns, with no more clothes than now cover myself; but, thank God, our lives are all spared, and within this breast is left a good Scottish heart, so I know we shall not want." '

These fires generally originate from the incautious burning of logs and boughs, which have been heaped together in some spot that has been recently cleared, the wood not being worth removing. A breeze perhaps springs up, and the adjoining trees catch fire, and then it is often impossible to arrest the flames.

Sometimes too, where the soil is peaty, it gets into the ground, and remains there smouldering for weeks beneath the surface. A gentleman told me of a fire in his father's land, which broke out in June. It remained in the ground during the following winter, burning beneath the snow, and burst out again in the spring! It is indeed a great mercy to have been spared witnessing such scenes.

One of my last drives was to Mansonville, which is one of our Missions, at the southern extremity of the Eastern Townships, and within a few miles of Lake Memphremagog. My wife and I started on Saturday morning in our waggon, and went over the hills to Abercorn, where I consecrated a Burial-ground, dined with some members of the

Church Mr. and Mrs. N——; and then on through a most lovely and romantic country to Glen Sutton. Here a little congregation was assembled for service in a schoolroom—a most primitive Service, and I preached to them on ' God is love.' We then proceeded to Mansonville, calling on our way on a nice old lady of eighty-four, who ' would very much like to see the Bishop.'

Next morning, Sunday, Mr. B—— and I went to South Bolton, which belongs to another Mission, and is now without a pastor. Here we had service at eleven, and returned through a beautiful country to Mansonville for an Evening Service, when the church was crammed. This is about the most Swiss-like portion of the country that we have passed through.

Our last pleasure excursion was to Eccles Hill, the scene of the recent conflict with the Fenians. We went a party of ten, and had a capital inspection of the battle-field. Dr. G—— and two Mr. B——s, who were in the engagement, were with us, and acted as excellent cicerones, pointing out to us all the interesting particulars.

It seems that, on the night before the skirmish, a party of the Home Guard (a small, but sturdy, band of Irregulars, composed of farmers in the neighbourhood of Dunham) occupied a little eminence close to the village of Eccles Hill. This ground is studded with rocks, which form a natural fortification. It is backed by a thick toll of trees, and commands the village and road, through which the Fenians were expected to pass.

The Home Guard was joined in the morning by about 200 Regular Volunteers. They all posted themselves in this strong and advantageous position; and presently the dreaded Fenians began to show themselves. A few advanced beyond the Border line, and were instantly fired upon by our men. Two or three fell, one in the road, about 300 yards off, and another as he was running across a field at about twice the distance. Several more were wounded, but escaped to a neighbouring wood, dying on the American side of the Border. In less than a quarter of an hour the work was done; and the Fenians, who did not expect so warm a reception, were glad enough to retire, never, I hope, to make another attempt to trouble us with their presence. Some of the regular troops, with Prince Arthur among them, were posted in the town of St. John's, ready to come to the rescue, had their aid been needed.

We saw the spot where one of the Fenians found a temporary grave; and we went into a house in the village, which had suffered a little from our rifle-balls. One of these had made a clean cut through a pane of glass, then through the opposite door, and lodging in the wall beyond.

We were very glad to have made this expedition before leaving the neighbourhood.

And now I must close my chapter, and the account of our pleasant stay in these country parts. Truly I may say of our good friends at Dunham, and indeed of the people of Canada generally, that their hospitality and kindness know no bounds. If a horse or a carriage is needed, you have but to name your want, and one is so cheerfully and willingly offered that you cannot refuse it; and as for food and lodging, they are at the service of every one, whether friend or stranger. During my year in Canada, in all my Visitation tours, which have been pretty numerous, I have *never once* had occasion to pay for a single article of food, or to provide for a conveyance. The clergy and laity seem to vie with each other in their kind and generous anxiety to serve their Bishop.

We closed most reluctantly our summer in the Eastern Townships, and I exchanged it for three weeks in the rougher parts of my Diocese. This however will not come into 'my First Year in Canada.'

CHAPTER IX.

STATUS AND PROSPECTS OF THE CHURCH.

I FOUND the Church, on my arrival, pretty well organised, with its Dean and Canons of the Cathedral, an Archdeacon, and four Rural Deans, besides some six or eight Honorary Canons. The staff of clergy amounted to about seventy. It had also its Synod for some years past, although its affairs were principally managed by a " Church Society." This society was however merged in the Synod shortly before my arrival. Thus I found the Church with its admirable and solid framework fully elaborated; and for this I am mainly indebted to the zeal, energy, and practical wisdom of my valued predecessor, Bishop Fulford. I have since added another Archdeacon to our staff.

The old Church Society seems to have done its work well for the time being. Still however it was but an imperfect organisation, and gave place to the Synod, which is the legitimate ruling power in the Church. The Church Society was suited to the days of the Church's pupilage ;

but the Synod belongs to a riper and more perfect system. The one was but a voluntary association within the Church ; whereas the other is the true representative Body of the Church itself.

The *Diocesan* Synod meets annually, and its sittings are generally extended over three or four days. The Bishop presides, and the members consist of all the licensed clergy, and lay delegates from the various parishes or missions, the whole number being upwards of two hundred.

The *Provincial* Synod, including representatives from the clergy and laity of the several dioceses, meets once in every three years, at Montreal. It consists of an Upper House of Bishops under the presidency of the Metropolitan, and a Lower House presided over by an elected Prolocutor The acts of this Synod rule the whole church of the Province.

The first Bishop of Canada, Dr. Mountain, was consecrated in 1793. Montreal was formed into a diocese, and Francis Fulford was consecrated its first Bishop, in 1856. The See is made over to the Bishop by Royal Patent, and he is regarded for all legal purposes as 'a corporation sole,' in whom is vested most of the Church property of the Diocese.

Each of the other Canadian Bishops is elected by the clergy and laity assembled in Synod. But the Bishop of Montreal, being also Metropolitan of the whole Province, is elected by a somewhat different process. The Synod of Montreal meets, and with it the House of Bishops ; and no election can be made by the Synod, unless the name is first sent down to them by the assembled Bishops.

The last election was nearly leading to a catastrophe. The Bishops named several for the office ; but one after another was rejected, either by the clergy or by the laity, whereas it was required that both should be consentients. A party in the Synod was anxious that some clergyman of the Diocese should be exalted to the Episcopate, and another party was equally determined that the office should be filled by a stranger. At one time, it seemed as if any solution whatever of the question was hopeless, until at length a compromise took place, and a reconciliation between the contending parties was happily effected.

The meeting of the Synod this year took place on Tuesday, June 21st, and we continued in session three days. It began as usual with a solemn service in the Cathedral, and a celebration of the Holy Communion. In the afternoon we met in the Synod room, where the names having been called over, and the officers appointed, I delivered an opening address,* and the Synod was fairly launched. Knowing the difficulties which had pre-

* *See* Appendix.

viously existed, I looked forward to its meeting
with some degree of apprehension ; but all went off
far better than I anticipated. The speaking was
short and to the point ; and although a little
party spirit every now and then showed itself, it
readily gave place to what was for the common
good.

On one or two occasions the gauntlet of discord
was thrown down ; but after a few explosive words
things went on calmly again. For example, the
introduction of the epithet *Protestant,* in framing
an address to the Irish Church, was the signal for
the discharge of a little oratorical artillery. A few
pungent words were uttered, and then all rallied
round the standard of peace. One speaker gloried
in the term Protestant ; another had rather have
his third finger amputated than that the word
should be expunged ; whilst a third contended,
that the Irish Church was not Protestant, but
Catholic. In our difficulty, when it seemed as
if some trouble must ensue, one of our moderate
and wise laymen, who has more than once before
come to the rescue on such occasions, and will,
I trust, do so yet again, stood up, and by a short,
but well-timed amendment succeeded in satisfying
the combatants on either side, and made each feel
that his own idiosyncrasy was truly represented.
It was indeed pleasant to see how a little brotherly
and Christian concession commended itself to all.

The most important measures were the adoption
of a Report on the future management of our
missions; also the selection of a certain number
of clerical, and an equal number of lay, delegates,
to represent our diocese at the next Provincial
Synod; and the appointment of thirty members
for the Executive Committee, in whom is vested
the management of all the fiscal affairs of the
diocese. These elections were made by ballot;
and the latter by the separate votes of clergy
and laity.

This arrangement of *voting by orders* is necessary
in this case, and is also resorted to on other special
occasions, on the application of any three members
of the House. This is an important safeguard
in cases where the peculiar interest of either order
is at stake; but, as it has a tendency to array
one body against the other, it is a privilege
which should be used very sparingly, and certainly
not for party purposes. There exists at present
a good feeling between the clerical and lay
members of our communion; and it is my earnest
and heartfelt wish that this feeling may be
strengthened; for without it the Church cannot
really prosper.

The annual meeting of the Synod is important,
as affording an opportunity for ventilating questions,
and for the expression of opinions, affecting the
welfare of the Diocese, and also for the framing of

canons for the due regulation of its Church work.
And this is done in a manner so consistent with
Church order that there is no room for discontent.

Besides the Synod meeting, we had in the
course of the winter another of scarcely less importance. It was the Annual Missionary Meeting
—not *Missionary* according to the English mean-
ing of the word—but in a Canadian sense, as it was
for the furtherance of general Church objects in the
various missions of the Diocese, and to give inform-
ation as to the progress of the work. The meeting
was a very successful one ; the room was crowded ;
and the speaking was unusually interesting and
effective. Some of our leading laymen took part
in it ; and we had upon the platform Bishop Stevens,
of Philadelphia, an able and eloquent representative
of our Sister Church in the United States. The
collection was larger and the numbers greater than
on former occasions ; and it gave, I trust, a little
spur to Church energy for the year.

And now what shall I say as to the prospects
of our beloved Church ? When I consider what
the Canadian Church was but a few years ago, and
what it is now, I do indeed rejoice and feel thankful. The present Dean of Montreal recollects the
first Anglican Bishop, and was himself ordained by
him. He began his Episcopate with only five

clergymen in the whole province : now we have about four hundred and fifty in the Province, and upwards of seventy in this Diocese. But we want more ; for there are fields here ripe for the harvest, if we had but labourers to occupy them. There are at this moment new Missions which ought to be opened, and which others will snatch from us if we do not seize our opportunity ; and there are clergymen working hard who are sadly overtaxed, and need help. I also long to employ one or two Travelling Missionaries, regularly to visit the Lumber Districts during the winter ; but we lack both men and funds. May some reader of these pages be stirred up either to offer himself for the work, or to give me the means of sending others ! Souls may thus be won, and members may be gathered into the Church.

Our Church system is fairly launched in its integrity. We have an able and devoted body of clergy, and a laity who feel a real interest in its welfare and prosperity. May God be with us, pouring out His Spirit upon each Mission, each minister, each member of the Church, and we shall then be blest, and be made a blessing to this land !

The Ecclesiastical Province, over which the Bishop of Montreal presides as Metropolitan, consists of the Dioceses of Huron, Toronto, Ontario, Montreal, and Quebec. But it is likely that the following will ere long be added ; Frederickton,

Nova Scotia, Newfoundland, Rupertsland, and Columbia.

The Church in the Diocese of Montreal derives no special advantages from the State, beyond the miserable pittance of 3500 dollars per annum, recovered with some difficulty from the Clergy Reserves, when they were secularized in 1855. She also retains six or seven Rectories, made over by Royal Patent. These however, as has been already shown, have scarcely any advantages over ordinary missions, and have no special salaries attached to them. The Rectory of Montreal is an exception, having the sum of three hundred pounds paid annually by the Government; but this will be forfeited at the death of the present Rector.

The income of the Church is derived from the following sources :—

1. From the small sum saved from the wreck of the Clergy Reserves;

2. From certain local Endowments;

3. From an annual Grant from the Society for the Propagation of the Gospel, which is gradually decreasing, and will eventually be withdrawn;

4. From the Voluntary Contributions of Church members.

From these sources, the wants of the Church are with difficulty supplied. When a mission is formed, the pecuniary capacity of the congregation is ascertained, and they pledge themselves to make up a certain sum, the remainder being supplemented by the General Church fund.

When a locality contributes but a third of the sum needed, the post is called a *Mission;* when one-half, it is a *Parish;* and when it becomes self-supporting, it is then considered as a *Rectory.* In the two first cases the Bishop appoints the clergy-man, whilst in the last the Congregation nominate him, and it rests with the Bishop to confirm the nomination if he approves.

The clergy are at present very inadequately paid, their incomes rarely exceeding 600 dollars, or a hundred and twenty pounds sterling. It would be greatly to the advantage of the Diocese, and to the credit of the Church, if a worthier stipend were accorded to those who 'labour in the word and doctrine.' If the clergy were thus relieved from the distracting cares of a straitened income, they would labour not only with more comfort, but with more power.

I have held three Ordinations during the past year, and have ordained seven clergymen. My first ordination was held in the Cathedral; my second at Hemmingford; and the third at Trinity Church, Montreal.

APPENDIX I.

FIRST SERMON IN THE CATHEDRAL, MONTREAL.

THE LORD'S CALL, AND MAN'S REPLY.—Isa. iv. 8.

'I heard the voice of the Lord, saying, Whom shall I send, and who will go for us? Then said I, Here am I, send me.'

THERE are times when the Lord calls upon His servants to enter upon some special work which He has marked out for them. He called upon Noah to prepare an ark for safety during the coming deluge. He called Abraham to quit his native country, and to shine like a beacon light in a distant land. He called Moses to give up a life of ease in the court of Pharaoh, and to undertake the leadership of His people Israel. He called Daniel to make a bold confession before the scoffers of Babylon. He called the sons of Zebedee to turn away from their seafaring life, and henceforward to become 'fishers of men.'

II

The case brought immediately before us in the text is perhaps still more special. We find the Lord condescending to invite His servants to volunteer, as it were, for a certain work on which His mind was bent. Like some great General, who sees that a fort is to be attacked, or a city wall to be scaled; so the Lord asks who of His soldiers will offer themselves for the enterprise He has in hand, and cries aloud, 'Whom shall I send, and who will go for us?' Upon which the prophet Isaiah steps forward with a willing heart; and without a moment's hesitation gives himself for the work; 'Here am I : send me.'

And yet, it may be, his heart was not altogether free from misgiving—not as to his *duty*, but as to his *fitness*. For do we not find him a moment before, when brought into the near presence of a holy God, shrinking back at the thought of his own shortcomings, and exclaiming, 'Woe is me, for I am undone, because I am a man of unclean lips; for mine eyes have seen the King, the Lord of hosts?' Yes, he was awed, not so much by the *difficulty* of the work to which the Lord might be pleased to call him, but from the persuasion of his own *inability* to discharge it—not that he felt *unwilling*, but *unworthy* to be employed for such a Master. 'Then (we are told) flew one of the Seraphims unto him, having a live coal from off the altar, and laid it upon his mouth, and said, Lo, this hath touched thy lips, and thine iniquity is taken away, and thy sin purged.'

And now, in a humbled and chastened spirit, but with a full assurance of God's pardoning mercy, and of his own acceptance, he stands boldly forward, ready for any errand to which he may be called.

Here, then, is a noble pattern for us to imitate. In the great machinery of God's world we have all of us a post to fill. God calls us to work for Him. It is true He does not *require* our aid; He can act wholly without us; but yet He graciously invites us to be workers together with Him. To each one He says, 'I have a work for you to do—a special work for which you are fitted—a work in which you may glorify me—a happy work in which it is your privilege to engage.' This work, whatever it be, may be small and insignificant in the eyes of men, or it may be great; it may be a work which needs self-denial; it may be a work unsought for, unlooked for. Still, if He summons you, and calls you to it, it is your duty and your happiness to enter upon it.

Some persons are always *looking out* for work, but never *finding* it. And yet perhaps their *real* work, that which God would have them engage in, lies all the while very plainly before them, but they see it not.

Some again are always *intending*, always *wishing* to do something for God ; and there it ends. Many things are thought of and talked about, but nothing is accomplished. Brethren, we must be *working*, and not mere *wishing* Christians ; *doers*, and not mere *dreamers*.

He says to us, ' Son, daughter, work to-day in My vineyard.' And woe unto us if we shrink from it ! Woe unto us, if we are slack and dilatory in obeying Him, if we put off till *to-morrow* what He bids us do *to-day !*

Then too some are ready to plead a backwardness arising from humility. ' What can *I* do in my humble position, situated as I am, with so few advantages, and so little influence ?' But surely we can all do *something* for our Lord. Does not our Master say, ' To every man his work ?' Whatever be your position, *something* is within your reach. Every one has an influence for good or evil which he may exert. Every one has a hand to lift, a foot to move, a heart to feel, a voice to raise. Every one may employ himself for the good of others and for God's glory. If through the mercy of God you have received light from above, you can let your light shine. You need not force it upon any one, but simply let it shine. Yes, and in God's sight your little speck of light may perhaps be as bright as the flaming torch of some great one. The smallest twinkling star above us is as precious to

Him, and in its measure serves His gracious purpose, as much as the brilliant mid-day sun.

Oh, that God would give us willing hearts! Oh, that we were more eager to labour for Him! Oh, that, when He says, ' Whom shall I send, and who will go for us?' we were ready to exclaim with all humility, but with a holy promptitude, ' Here am I: send me.' ' Lord, what wilt Thou have me to do?'

It is a great mercy, Brethren, when God shows us clearly where our work lies, when He points the way so plainly and unmistakably that we can but follow. Thank God this seemed to be the case with myself, when suddenly and unexpectedly a call came to me from this Church in Canada to leave the quiet and humble post that I was filling, and to occupy the exalted position which is now assigned to me. A call so distinct from the Church of Christ, gathered in solemn Synod, seemed also to be a clear call from God ; and I could not— dared not—hesitate. It whispered, as it were, in accents too clear to be mistaken, ' Son, go work to-day in another portion of My vineyard. The time is short. Life's little hour will soon be gone. The sun has passed its meridian ; ere it sets, go forth and work awhile in a new field of labour. My finger points the way. My everlasting arm supports thee. My presence shall go with thee.'

Could I then hold back ? Could I hesitate to

accept a call so lovingly made ? Instead of taking credit for any willingness to obey, I should have been simply faithless had I doubted.

And now I proceed upon my errand, conscious of the important task which I have undertaken, but assured that He who has called me to it can also fit me for it. Feeling that the discharge of a humbler office in the Church would perhaps have been better suited to my powers, but knowing that He can give me grace and strength even for the highest.

And now, dear Brethren, I want your *Sympathy*, your *Help*, your *Prayers*.

I want your *Sympathy ;* and I feel that I shall have it. Are we not 'One body in Christ, and everyone members one of another ? ' Are we not children of a common Father, and servants of the same loving Saviour ? Are not the interests of one the interests of us all ? Are we not as sheaves bound up in the same bundle of life, placed one here and another there in the wide harvest field, but to be gathered one day into the same heavenly garner ? One of the gospel's golden rules is that we should ' bear one another's burdens, and so fulfil the law of Christ.' And truly this rule has been abundantly observed towards me. I may say that there are few things that have tended more to sweeten the bitterness of parting with those most dear to us in our own beloved land, than the marvellous sympathy which has been so abundantly shown us both by friends and strangers.

Never, I think, has anyone been blest with so many kind and affectionate wishes as I have experienced in the last few weeks—the hearty expression of good will from both rich and poor, who have desired to speed us on our way. These have been like sweet breezes which have wafted me and mine to the shores of our adopted country. These *have* comforted us in our moments of trial ; and the grateful remembrance of these *will* comfort us in days to come.

And, thanks be to God, we find that self-same spirit of affection awaiting us here—throwing open, as it were, its arms to receive us. Though we have exchanged a long-cherished home, and still dearer ties, for those which are altogether new, we rejoice to find that the strong but invisible thread of sympathy is in no way severed ; but we still feel its sustaining power ; it still draws us out of ourselves, and binds us on to those whose faces are strange to us, but whose hearts are one with us.

But, further, I want your *Help*. And I am asking you for what you all may give me. In a family the humblest servant or the youngest child may be very helpful to his Master or his Parent. In a parish each individual member of the flock may give a helping hand to his Minister. He may help him by his influence; for who is there that has not, as I said just now, *some* influence? Who is there that may not *say* something, or *do* something, to forward the great work in which his pastor is engaged? He may help him by following his directions and carrying out his plans. He may help him yet more by the daily preaching of a holy and consistent life. And, Brethren, as your Bishop, I also shall look to you for help. The work I have undertaken is a very arduous one; but you, each one of you, may do something to lighten it. I cannot tell you how much it will tend to diminish my burden, if I can have the happy feeling that you are doing your best—it may be but little, but still your best—to strengthen my hands and cheer my heart. I shall doubtless have my trials and my difficulties. Some will blame me for being too severe; others for being too remiss. There are those whose quick eye will be ready to mark each little error in judgment, each inconsistency in conduct; for who among us can always stand upright; who is there that has not need to pray, 'Cleanse thou me from secret faults?' But at such times of trial and difficulty, when my heart will perhaps ache within me, and my path for a moment will be full of perplexity, and the feeling that I have done my very best will not be enough to reassure me, if I can fall back upon the kind forbearance of my brethren, the charity that thinketh no evil, the love that is ever ready to start up in support of God's servants, then I shall indeed feel that I have a tower of strength, on which I can confidently rely.

And yet, after all, whether in the case of a parent, or of a minister, or of one filling a still higher post, in every time of anxiety our truest refuge is in God, our real repose is in the bosom of our Lord. Happy indeed is he who can look up and say, 'Thou art my hiding-place;' 'Thou wilt keep him in perfect peace whose mind is stayed on Thee.'

I ask then for your Help; and I have shown you that you can give it. I shall greatly need it in carrying out my plans for the good of the Diocese. I shall need it, if I am to accomplish anything here for God. I shall need it, for my own comfort and encouragement. Alone, I shall be weak and powerless; but, backed and supported by you, I shall feel a strength which will sustain me.

But I have another request to make, a yet *harder* request to grant, a boon even *more* difficult to bestow. I want your Prayers—not a *momentary* lifting up of your hearts for me, but a *continued* pleading in my behalf before God, who can make me all that He would have me to be. Pray, Brethren, that I may have come to you in the fulness of the blessing of the Gospel of Peace. Pray that He who has summoned me to my exalted post may strengthen me and guide me in the discharge of it. Plead for one who greatly needs help from above— grace in his own soul—and vigour to nerve him for his work. Pray that a living fire may touch my lips, and that the Holy Spirit of God may sanctify my heart. The prayers of Abraham would have saved the guilty cities, steeped as they were in iniquity, had there been but ten righteous men in them. Elijah's prayer called down refreshing showers on the parched plains of Israel. Prayer helped St. Paul in his abundant labours. And, Brethren, if you wish to help *me*, pray for me, that my labour may not be in vain in the Lord. In answer to your prayers, souls may be saved, and gifts may descend, like the former and latter rain, upon the thirsty ground. 'Prove me now herewith, saith the Lord, if I will not open the windows of heaven, and pour you out a blessing, that there shall not be room enough to receive it.'

Be assured, God has great things to give, and He loves to give them in answer to our entreaties. He will be inquired of for this to do it for us. 'The effectual, fervent prayer of a righteous man '— of even the humblest servant of God—'availeth much.'

And now, before I close my sermon—my first sermon preached in this my Diocese—let me express a fervent wish that God's best blessing may rest upon this branch of the Church of England; that she may ever be a living, growing, advancing Church; that she may be sound in faith and holy in practice; wise in her moderation, and yet abounding in zeal and earnestness; that she may be faithful, devoted, and true to her Lord. Oh, that God may bless her clergy, and give spiritual life and grace to all her members!

Beloved, I now commend you to God, and to the word of His grace, praying that He will build up those among you who are His true people, and enable you to walk more and more closely with Him; praying, also, that He may be pleased, by the power of His Holy Spirit, to draw those of you to Himself who as yet know Him not and love Him not; so that you too may be numbered among His children now, and enjoy His presence hereafter for ever.

APPENDIX II.

PRIMARY ADDRESS TO THE MEMBERS OF THE SYNOD.

MY BRETHREN OF THE CLERGY AND LAITY,—In presiding for the first time over this your Annual Synod, I must ask you to bear with me if I begin with a few remarks personal to myself.

Having been summoned by the unanimous vote of the Clerical and Lay representatives of the Church in this Diocese, when solemnly assembled in Synod, I felt that I had no alternative but to leave my quiet retreat in England, where I had watched over a simple and affectionate people for one-and-twenty years, to obey at once your call, and to come among you as your elected Bishop.

I felt that under such circumstances your call was the echo, as it were, of a higher summons from above; and I regarded the expression of your wishes as indicative of the will of God. I came out therefore to fill my allotted post, not without sundry misgivings, but at the same time with a

strongly impressed conviction, and I may also say
with an assured confidence, that He, who seemed
so plainly to have marked out my path, and who
Himself knew all my deficiencies, would give me
the needed strength, the requisite wisdom, and the
grace to fit me for my new and unexpected work.

During the ten months that I have exercised
my episcopal office among you, I may truly say
that I have never once regretted the step which I
have taken. The kind and generous reception
which I met with on my first arrival from the inhabitants of this city and Diocese ; the cordial and
affectionate desire shown by the Clergy to carry out
my wishes ; and the very hearty co-operation of the
Laity, who have evinced a zeal for the Church's
welfare, as well as a respect for my office, which at
once endears them to me—these would of themselves be sufficient to call forth my thankfulness, and
make me content with my present lot. But I have
yet further cause for gratitude from the marked way
in which God has, in answer to my prayers, been
graciously pleased to endue me with bodily
strength, such as I have not experienced for years
past, and to afford me other helps to fit me for the
emergencies of my new position. To Him I desire
thus publicly to give the praise.

I cannot help taking this early opportunity of
acknowledging the debt I owe to my justly revered
and beloved Predecessor, for the great work he

achieved, with your assistance, in laying the foundation, and building up to its present height, the
Church in this Diocese, with all its synodical and
other organization. It is indeed a glorious structure,
which will ever bear the impress of his wisdom, his
intelligence, and his Christian character. He has
been the 'wise Master Builder ;' and it remains for
his successors to rear the spiritual edifice, according
to the model which he has designed with such
consummate care and skill. There are many
features in our Canadian Church system, especially
as regards its synodical character, which have
called forth the unqualified admiration of our
brethren in the mother country. And all that we
now want is from time to time the infusion of fresh
life into it, that life of which the Holy Spirit is
alone the Author and Giver.

And now there are certain points of general
interest, in connexion with our Church and Diocese,
which I desire to touch upon.

1. First, as regards our *Country Missions.**

The number of these amounts at the present
time to fifty-nine, having many of them from two
to four churches or congregations attached to them.
Of these I regret to say only eight are self-supporting, and the remaining fifty-one are more or

* These should perhaps rather be called 'Church Stations,' since many of them have lately assumed a less
missionary, and a more permanent, character.

less dependent on the Church at large for their maintenance. It is essential that these should be properly and vigorously sustained, that the ministerial teaching in each mission should be efficient, the public services adequate, and our admirable Church system heartily carried out.

But our attention must not be confined to *existing* missions. Whilst we use every exertion to preserve *these* in a flourishing condition, we must also be constantly on the alert to occupy fresh fields of labour as they present themselves. And I am persuaded that if our Church has real life and vigour in her, her bounds will be extending themselves year by year; and though an increased demand will thereby be made upon her resources, she will hail with joy every fresh necessity as it arises to multiply her missions, and increase her staff of labourers.

There are at this time two or three new posts, which might with advantage be entered upon, in each of which a faithful missionary would find his labours abundantly rewarded; and each of which, if not undertaken by ourselves, will eventually be lost to the Church. There is also great need for two 'Travelling Missionaries,' to visit the lumber districts during the winter months, and to carry to those hardy and endurant men the message of the Gospel and the ministrations of the Church.

May we not look forward to such an increase

in our resources as will enable us to carry out these works of faith and labours of love, and that devoted men will not be wanting to fill these posts of self-denial to which the Church calls them?

In providing for the spiritual wants of our members, we should have a due regard for those districts which cry out to us for help, but can bring little or no resources of their own to supply the stipends of their ministers. To refuse to establish a new mission simply because there is but little prospect of its being in any measure self-supporting, would be a fatal error. To despise a call from our brethren because they chance to be poor would be contrary to the spirit of the gospel, and be unwise as well as unchristian. The fact of the Church's ministrations being demanded should be a sufficient reason for supplying that demand, if practicable, at any sacrifice to ourselves. There is much truth in the remark which I have somewhere seen, that 'a Church which is content to lose its poor is losing its true riches.'

And this leads me to speak of the manner in which our missions are at present sustained. The Church's work in this Diocese is to a certain extent fettered for lack of funds. Now, if it is to be carried on in a really earnest and hearty spirit, as I trust it will be, these five things are needed:

First, Our Church members in the various parishes must make a more strenuous effort to supply *their* proportion of the stipends of the Clergy who labour among them. I know that many of them can ill afford to do this, but I am very sure that they will see the paramount necessity of giving to the very utmost of their means for an object in which they themselves are so deeply interested.

Secondly, The richer Laity of the Church, in this city and elsewhere, must be prepared for an increased demand upon their contributions to the General Church Fund of the Diocese; or, I would suggest (what would be far more beneficial) that they be willing, as some have already done, to name a *fixed annual sum* as their regular subscription to the fund. Their past liberality, whenever appealed to, makes me feel the most entire confidence that it will not be withheld, if only it be clearly shown to them that their Church needs it.

Thirdly, In addition to the requirement of the Synod that an annual sermon be preached in every Church, it will be necessary that a *bonâ fide* collection be made from house to house in every parish or mission throughout the Diocese, in augmentation of this general fund.

Fourthly, It will be necessary that an enquiry be made into the state of the various Endowments which exist in certain parishes, and the manner in which each property is invested; also that a correct record be kept by the registrar of all such endowments.

Fifthly, And above all, a better organization is required for the distribution of our mission funds. I am rejoiced to say that a committee of laymen has been sitting, for the purpose of remodelling our system of grants on the one hand, and our requirements for the people on the other. Whatever changes this committee may recommend in their report, and the Synod may sanction, will, I trust, be carried out with the hearty concurrence of both clergy and laity.

It is the more necessary that the Mission Fund should be forthwith placed on a sound footing, since the Society for the Propagation of the Gospel is gradually withdrawing its hitherto liberal grant from the Church in this colony.

I feel that there is yet another point which I dare not omit. I believe that no Church will thoroughly prosper, unless she enlarge her heart towards those nations which enjoy not the same spiritual blessings as herself. While trying then to meet our own pressing needs, we must not close our hearts towards those of our fellow-men who are sitting in darkness and the shadow of death. Let us make an effort, according to our means, to extend help to others, and then we may look for God's blessing on ourselves. 'There is that scattereth, and yet increaseth.'

During the past year the special collections throughout the Diocese have been carried on with much zeal, and with some success. The Annual Meeting, in the Mechanics' Hall, was perhaps the largest that has been held for many years. And we were glad to number among the pleaders for our work an eminent Bishop of the American Church. By his eloquence, the cause of our mission was greatly advanced; and also an opportunity was given for the interchange of those cordial and brotherly feelings, which will, I trust, ever exist between the two Churches— each carefully adapting itself to the special require- ments of its position, but both one, indissolubly one, in all essential matters of faith and practice.

> ' Facies non omnibus una,
> Nec diversa tamen, qualem decet esse sororum.' ·

Whilst speaking on the subject of our financial resources, it will not, I trust, be thought out of place if I allude to a method very much resorted to at the present time, in order to raise money for religious objects—I mean that of *Bazaars.* I am quite aware of the multifarious and pressing nature of those efforts which, from time to time, claim the attention of clergymen and others. I am aware too of the exceeding difficulty of obtaining funds for the accomplishment of any good object. But still the end, however desirable,

can never sanctify the means, if in themselves
unworthy. It seems to me that by so doing we
are setting aside real Christian benevolence, as
if it were a thing in these days hardly to be
attained, and are substituting in its stead a
spurious and worldly system of liberality, on
which God's blessing can scarcely be expected
or even asked for. I should be very thankful to
see a higher standard of almsgiving, and a healthier
tone of charity, prevailing among the members
of our Church.

But I now pass on to speak, secondly, of the
Condition and Prospects of our Clergy.

I have on another public occasion borne my
willing testimony to the general character of those
who minister in holy things among us. I doubt if
there is any Bishop who can boast of a more la-
borious, self-denying, earnest clergy than those who
are working under my episcopal superintendence.

I cannot but speak with much thankfulness
of the general harmony of views which exists
among us, and of the soundness, faithfulness, and
moderation, which for the most part mark the
preaching from our pulpits. There will ever be
some few whose opinions reach the extreme line
of what the Church permits; but I am not aware
of any within my Diocese who are so decidedly
overstepping that line as to call for my interference.

Still there are some, whom I would gladly see conforming more heartily to the general feeling and spirit of the Church in which they serve. And I am extremely anxious that, by a little modification of practice, and by the exercise of a conciliatory spirit, there may be brought about a more entire conformity throughout the Diocese, especially in the ordinary mode of conducting our services. I hope that those who feel with me in this matter will be willing to make a sacrifice of their own cherished opinions, where at least no sacred principle is involved, in order to attain this desirable end ; and that they will boldly lead the way in making such concessions.

It is the policy of our great enemy to separate us from one another as widely as he can ; it should be *our* policy—our holy and Christian policy— to close our ranks, and wage our warfare side by side. Our strength lies in united action. And if God is pleased to draw us nearer together by the attraction of a loving spirit, this will make us strong against our common foe, and strong in the discharge of our spiritual mission. May it ever be so with us ! For then, and not otherwise, will our Church answer to that description given in the inspired song; she will be 'beautiful as Tirzah, comely as Jerusalem, terrible as an army with banners.'

As regards our Christian brethren who belong

to other communions, we should avoid anything like an attitude of antagonism towards them, or the use of hard words and unkind expressions, whilst we hold our own with a honest and firm hand. We should inculcate in our teaching sound and definite Church principles, and at the same time set forth clearly, distinctly, and prominently, the great and life-giving doctrines of the Cross. Our best weapon is, I believe, an earnest declaration of what we know to be God's truth, a simple uplifting of Christ before our people, and a desire to embody this teaching in our daily lives.

On the appointment of a clergyman to any leading parish or mission, I propose in future either to induct him into his charge myself in the presence of the whole congregation, or to commission some one of my clergy to act as my representative in so doing. The entrance of a clergyman into a new sphere of labour, and his reception by the congregation, I feel to be of so solemn a nature, that the opening service in which he takes part ought to be marked by some public ceremony befitting the occasion. I have prepared a Form of Service for this purpose, which is chiefly borrowed from one in use in the Sister Church of America.

I spoke just now of the duty and expediency of sustaining our *Missions* with vigour. But we must not forget that the Church has also a duty to perform towards the *Labourers* in these missions. The incomes of the clergy strike me as being lamentably small; not merely in comparison with the stipends allotted to them in other dioceses, but also in comparison with those enjoyed by men who are engaged in other and less important callings. Many of our most active clergymen are at present receiving barely $600 a-year. I am glad however to see it acknowledged in the authorized rules and constitution of the Church in this Diocese, that 'the minimum salary of the clergy shall be $800 per annum.' I should be still more glad if that intention could be *carried out*, though at present it seems scarcely possible, owing to the deficient state of our funds. I would express a hope that the attention of the laity will be directed to this urgent question ; and the more so, as I feel assured that no request will emanate from the clergy themselves.

The fact that the supply of clergymen is at present somewhat below the demand is attributable in part to this inadequacy of the remuneration we have to offer them. It is true, men can be found, but not men of the right stamp, to fill our ranks. And I am sure you will agree with me in feeling that it would be a serious disaster to our Church, if, in consequence of the lack of men, we were to lower the qualifications of our clergy, and admit candidates of an inferior grade. My desire is to raise, if possible, the standard of ministerial efficiency, rather than to diminish it, assured that in these days especially we want a well-educated, as well as an earnest and faithful, body of clergy.

The number of spiritual labourers within the Diocese at this time amounts to eighty-seven. Of these seventy-nine are in holy orders, and the remaining eight are catechists, or lay readers, licensed by the Bishop.

3. The *Training of our Candidates for Holy Orders* is not altogether on a satisfactory footing. The fact of our Theological College being at a distance places us at a disadvantage. And I should certainly be thankful if I could gather my candidates for the sacred ministry around me here at Montreal, where I could watch their characters and conduct, and superintend their preparation for the ministry. I feel unwilling however without more mature consideration to interfere with the present arrangement as regards the college at Lennoxville. But if it should eventually be found desirable to move the theological department nearer home, I doubt not that I should obtain from the Churchmen of the Diocese the needed help to enable me to carry out the project. My present conviction is that, if we had in this city

a Theological Institution, with a Building worthy
of its character, it would prove an immense blessing
to the Diocese.

4. I feel anxious to take this opportunity of
calling attention to what I consider a very lax
and objectionable practice in administering the
Sacrament of *Baptism*, and in celebrating the rite
of *Marriage*, in private houses. There are reasons
why it should have been permitted in this country,
and principally from the fact of many parishes
having been hitherto unprovided with Churches.
These reasons however for the most part no
longer exist. I must request my clergy to dis-
continue a practice so entirely without precedent
in our Church, except in peculiar cases, and then
not without the special permission of the Diocesan.
As regards Baptism, however, the illness of the
recipient is, of course, a sufficient ground for the
use of the private service provided in our prayer
book.

5. The subject of *Liturgical Changes* has of late
occupied some attention. I have on many occasions, both in the Convocation of Canterbury and
elsewhere, advocated a certain modification of our
rubrical directions, to suit the wants of the present
generation. I would gladly see liberty given for
the use of the Morning Prayer, the Litany, and the

office for the Holy Communion, as separate services, according to the original intention; or, when used in their combined form, divested of certain repetitions which now mar their beauty.

We greatly need also *a Third Form of Service*, to be used in the evening in those churches where prayers have already been read in the morning and afternoon. This seems to be especially called for in our city congregations.

And further, we perhaps want *a curtailed Form of Prayer* for occasional or special use.

But for these we may be well content to wait, until the Mother Church leads the way, which she is evidently prepared to do at no very distant day.

I much hope that the new *Lectionary*, which has been prepared with great care by the Ritual Commission, and has passed the English Convocation, will be submitted to our Provincial Synod at its next meeting. The adoption of this new Calendar of Lessons will be a great boon to our Church, and has long been wanted.

I propose putting into the hands of my clergy *a Form of Harvest Thanksgiving*. It may be used this year merely as an optional service, with a view to some approved Form being ultimately submitted to the Provincial Synod for its sanction.

6. The expediency of having one authorised

Hymn Book for the Diocese, if not for the whole Province, has been much on my mind. A committee appointed by the Provincial Synod upon the subject is now sitting, and will, I hope, before next year be prepared with its Report.

There are many difficulties and arguments which array themselves against the adoption of such a book, but the countervailing advantages seem to me to be immense.

I have long felt that the lack of uniformity in this respect is a prominent source of the Church's weakness; and I should heartily rejoice to see it remedied. We are rich in Hymn-books in the present day; and from the varied treasures that exist an excellent selection may be made, and one that would, I hope, commend itself to persons of all views, and would meet with general acceptance. In any case it would be very unwise to make the reception of such a book *compulsory* on our congregations: it would be sufficient that its introduction into the diocese or province should be *permissive*, sanctioned as it would be by authority.

7. I cannot omit the mention of a subject which has given rise to some discussion in the lesser meetings of our Clergy and Laity. I refer to *the Ruri-diaconal System.*

I know that it has not found much favour with the Clergy generally; but feeling that the office is of ancient origin, and that it now forms an integral part of our Ecclesiastical system, feeling also that it may be made extremely helpful to the Bishop, as well as conducive to the good order and working of the Diocese, I am unwilling lightly to abandon it. I must therefore ask you to bear with me in my conservative wish that it should be continued as a part of our Church Organization. I propose however in the event of vacancies occurring, to leave the selection of the Rural Dean in a great measure in the hands of the Clergy of the Deanery. This will relieve me of some responsibility, and make me feel that the office is filled by one of your own choice. It may also be desirable to review and re-cast the Form of Instructions given to the Rural Dean, on his appointment by the Bishop.

8. I am thankful to say that I have been enabled to visit the larger half of the Diocese, namely, forty-three missions, during the past ten months ; and I hope to complete my visitation of the whole before the commencement of another winter. My first Episcopal act was to consecrate the little church at Como in September last. Other churches are now in the course of erection : and several, especially in the Deanery of St. Andrews, will be ready for consecration during the ensuing. autumn. I have held Confirmations in twenty

parishes, and received nearly four hundred persons into full membership with the Church. I have also ordained six Clergymen, who are now at work in the Diocese.

And now, as to the future of our beloved Church in this land, I cannot but think that the prospect is bright and hopeful. With a sound and devoted Clergy, loving the work which their Heavenly Master has given them to do, and anxious by the power of His Holy Spirit to win souls to Him; and with a generous and right-hearted laity, zealous not merely for their own, but for the Church's welfare, we have little to fear. There is a great and glorious work entrusted to us by our Lord; and happy for us if during our short hour of life we take, each of us, our part in the fulfilment of it. On you, my reverend brethren, devolves the important duty of acting as leaders in the progress onward; and whilst you go forward, undaunted by the difficulties before you, and confiding in the promise of your Lord, sure I am that our lay brethren will rally round you, upholding you in your great enterprise by their untiring aid, and cheering you by their sympathy.

I have now only a few more words to add regarding the present Synod, which I have to-day the privilege of opening, and over which I have the still greater privilege of presiding. I have looked forward to its meeting with some degree of anxiety, knowing the influence which its calm and dignified bearing will have upon the Church at large, and feeling the great responsibility of the part in it which I am called to take. But of this I am assured, that if He whose aid we have solemnly invoked, is Himself with us, my anxiety will be exchanged for thankfulness. The eyes of many of our brother Churchmen are turned towards Canada at the present time ; let it be seen, from the temper we display at our Synod meetings, that we can come together as Christian brethren, and separate with our hearts warmed, and our spirits calmed and chastened.

I am inclined to think that in all mixed gatherings of Churchmen there is some little danger, lest a feeling of clanship should be allowed to spring up between the Clergy and Laity. This should be especially guarded against ; for surely the interests of the one body are the interests also of the other ; and the moment those interests are divided, the well-being of the Church is in peril of being weakened.

It is for this reason that I would venture to recommend a very sparing use of our privilege of *Voting by Orders.* It is important for both parties that the privilege exists ; but we should resort to it only on very exceptional occasions. This manner of voting should be regarded by us as something rather held in reserve, than brought into frequent exercise—as a power which should be rather felt, than often used. It is well for a Church when its clerical and lay members feel such mutual confidence towards each other, that they can consult together with perfect freedom and singleness of purpose. And better still is it when they can be seen habitually voting together, and acting together, without distinction. This should be our rule; the other only the rare exception.

And may I not also express a hope, an earnest hope, that the *Clerical* members of this Synod may have come here prepared to lay aside their sectional differences—that from the tone which prevails within these walls it may be happily apparent to all that the spirit of party is speedily dying out, and that the spirit of union is taking its place.

Try to forget, my Reverend Brethren, any little specialties, either of doctrine or practice, which have in days past ranged you on separate sides ; and think only of the greatness of those matters on which you are sent here to deliberate, and of His honour which should be dearer to you than all else. Look at each question which shall come before you, not as to how it will affect yourselves, but how it will affect the Church at large.

In your recent Sessions the subject which engaged your attention was of an unusually exciting character, and naturally aroused a certain warmth of feeling. That subject has now passed away, and with it I trust any little irritation which it called up at the time. We shall henceforth do well to lay aside all bitterness of feeling, and devote ourselves to those questions of practical importance which shall come before us. And surely if our deliberations are conducted in a spirit of self-control, and as in the presence of God Himself—if we speak with all deference towards each other, and with due respect for the opinions of those who may chance to differ from us—then may opposing views be expressed without the slightest risk of our harmony being disturbed.

I have full confidence in those who are now before me, that they will strive to promote the feeling which I have expressed; and that their chief forbearance will be exercised towards myself, in presiding for the first time over this important Assembly.

May the Holy Spirit so possess our hearts with His calm and gracious influence, that we may speak with all Christian love and wisdom! And may He Himself so direct all that shall be said and done during this present session, that it may tend to the advancement of His glory, and the growth of His Kingdom among us!

London : STRANGEWAYS AND WALDEN, Printers, Castle St., Leicester Sq.

WORKS BY
THE RT. REV. ASHTON OXENDEN, D.D.

Bishop of Montreal and Metropolitan of Canada.

PUBLISHED BY HATCHARDS, 187 PICCADILLY.

---

1. Short Lectures on the Sunday Gospels.

Two Vols. { VOL. I. ADVENT TO EASTER.
{ VOL. II. EASTER TO ADVENT.

Lately published. Tenth Thousand. Fcap. cloth, large type, each
2s 6d.

2. The Christian Life.

16th Thousand. Enlarged, fcap. cloth, large type, 2s. 6d. morocco, 7s.

3. The Pathway of Safety; or, Counsel to the

AWAKENED. 175th Thousand. Fcap. cloth, 2s. 6d.; morocco, 7s.

4. The Parables of our Lord.

Nineteenth Thousand. Fcap. cloth, 3s.

5. Our Church and her Services.

Eighteenth Thousand. Fcap. cloth, 2s. 6d.

6. Decision.

Tenth Thousand. 18mo. cloth, 1s. 6d.

7. Family Prayers (For Four Weeks).

By the BISHOP OF MONTREAL and the REV. C. H. RAMSDEN.
60th Thousand. Fcap. 2s. 6d.; morocco, 7s.

8. Prayers for Private Use.

48th Thousand. Fcap. limp cloth, 1s.; limp calf or morocco, 3s. 6d.

9. Portraits from the Bible. Old Testament

SERIES, containing Thirty-three Sketches of Bible Characters.
Twenty-sixth Thousand. Fcap. cloth. 3s.

10. **Portraits from the Bible.** New Testament
SERIES, containing Thirty-four Sketches of Bible Characters.
Fourteenth Thousand. Fcap. cloth, 3s.

11. **The Pastoral Office** : its Duties, Privileges,
and PROSPECTS. Third Edition. Fcap. cloth, 3s. 6d.

12. **Cottage Sermons**; or, Plain Words to the
POOR. Fifth Thousand. Fcap. cloth, 3s.

13. **Cottage Readings.** Fcap. cloth, 3s. 6d.

14. **Words of Peace** ; or, The Blessings and Trials
OF SICKNESS. Thirty-fifth Thousand. Fcap. cloth, 1s. 6d.

15. **The Home Beyond** ; or, a Happy Old Age
Ninetieth Thousand. Fcap. cloth, large type, 1s. 6d.

16. **Fervent Prayer.**
Twenty-ninth Thousand. 18mo. cloth, 1s. 6d.

17. **The Story of Ruth.**
Ninth Thousand. 18mo. cloth. 1s. 6d.

18. **God's Message to the Poor.**
Sixteenth Thousand. 18mo. cloth, 1s. 6d.

19. **The Labouring Man's Book.**
Thirty-eighth Thousand. 18mo cloth, 1s. 6d.

20. **Baptism Simply Explained.**
Eighth Thousand. 18mo. limp cloth, 1s.

21. **The Lord's Supper Simply Explained.**
Thirty-second Thousand. 18mo. limp cloth, 1s.

22. **The Earnest Communicant.** A Course
OF PREPARATION FOR THE LORD'S TABLE. 190th
Thousand. 18mo. limp cloth, 1s. ; limp calf or morocco, 3s. 6d.

23. **A Plain History of the Christian Church.**
Sixth Thousand. 18mo. limp cloth, 1s.

24. **Great Truths in very Plain Language.**
Twenty-sixth Thousand. 18mo. cloth, 1s.

25. **Confirmation**; or, Are You Ready to Serve
CHRIST? 230th Thousand. 18mo. sewed, 3d : cloth limp, 6d.

BARHAM TRACTS.

25 for 1s. 4d. assorted, or the 49 numbers in packet, 3s.

No.	d.
1. The Bible	1
2. Prayer	1
3. Public Prayer	1
4. Family Prayer	1
5. Cottage Family Prayers	2
Ditto, in covers	3
6. The Sinner and the Saviour	1
7. Are you Happy?	1
8. Are you Ready?	1
9. Passion Week	2
10. Baptism; or, What is the good of being Christened?	1
11. The Lord's Supper; or, Who are the Welcome Guests?	1
12. My Duty to my Child	1
13. How shall I Spend Sunday?	1
14. The Season of Sickness	1
15. The Great Journey	1
16. How shall I spend Christmas?	1
17. I am deaf, and therefore do not go to Church	1
18. The Prayer which many use, and but few understand	1
19. Old John; or, the Bible with a large Print	1
20. Is my State a safe one?	1
21. Poor Sarah	1
22. The Holy Spirit	1
23. A Happy New Year	1
24. A Word or two about Lent	1
25. How shall I spend Whitsuntide?	1

No.	d.
26. Private Prayers for Cottagers	1
27. How shall I spend To-day?	
28. What shall I do this Michaelmas?	1
29. The Fatal Railway Accident	1
30. A Word or Two for Servants	1
31. My Duty to the Heathen	1
32. The Promised Land	1
33. I have had my Child registered	1
34. What can I do for my Church and my Parish?	1
35. Thoughts for the Sick and Sorrowful	2
36. The Pathway through the Corn-field	1
37. Simple Truth for the Unlearned	1
38. Do you believe the Bible?	1
39. True and False Repentance	1
40. David Jones; or, the old Welsh Churchman	1
41. Alfred Barton; or, the Down-hill Path	1
42. The Great Deliverer	1
43. The Joyful Resurrection	
44. Heavenward. A Tract for Ascension Day	1
45. Deathbeds	1
46. The *Sleeping* Sinner on Earth	1
47. The *Awakened* Sinner in Hell	1
48. The *Penitent* Sinner on Earth	1
49. The *Saved* Sinner in Heaven	1

PLUCKLEY TRACTS. (First Series.)

25 for 1s. 4d. assorted, or the 33 numbers in packet, 2s.

No.	d.
1. Adam; or the Forfeited Inheritance	1
2. Cain and Abel; or, the Infidel and the True Believer	1
3. Enoch; or, a Close Walk with God	1
4. Methuselah; or, Life's Pilgrimage	1
5. Noah; or, the Preaching Life	1
6. Abraham; or, Faith and Works	1
7. Lot; or, the Unhappy Choice	1
8. Isaac; or, the Child of Promise	1
9. Jacob; or, the Wrestler with God	1
10. Joseph; or, the Secret of True Prosperity	1

No.	d.
11. Job; or, the Blessing of Affliction	1
12. Moses; or, the Faithful Leader	1
13. Pharaoh; or, the Gradual Hardening of the Heart	1
14. Balaam; or, the Empty Wish	1
15. Joshua; or, the Pious Officer	1
16. Samson; or, Man's Weakness and God's Strength	1
17. Ruth; or, the Mourner Comforted	1
18. Eli; or, Mistaken Kindness	1
19. Samuel; or, the Son of many Prayers	1
20. Saul; or, Misery in the midst of Greatness	1

No.	d.	No.	d.
21. David; or, the Man after God's own Heart	2	28. Daniel; or, the Safety of those who Trust God	1
22. Solomon; or, Grace is Better than Wisdom	1	29. Shadrach, Meshach, and Abednego; or, Deliverance in the Midst of Danger	1
23. Elijah; or, the Fearless Man of God	1	30. Jonah; or, the Withered Gourd	1
24. Elisha; or, the Lowly Exalted	1	31. Belshazzar; or, the Handwriting on the Wall	1
25. Hezekiah; or, the Good King	1	32. Nehemiah; or, Prayer the Secret of Success	1
26. Manasseh; or, the Royal Penitent	1	33. Haman; or, the Favourite Disgraced	1
27. Josiah; or, the Right-minded King	1		

PLUCKLEY TRACTS. (Second Series.)

25 for 1s. 4d. assorted, or the 34 numbers in packet, 2s.

No.	d.	No.	d.
1. St. John the Baptist; or, the Voice in the Wilderness	1	19. Cornelius; or, the First-fruits from among the Gentiles	1
2. Simeon; or, the Aged Believer	1	20. Onesimus; or, the Converted Slave	1
3. Andrew; or, the True-hearted Brother	1	21. St. John; or, the Disciple whom Jesus Loved	1
4. St. Peter; or, Strength and Weakness. Part I.	1	22. The Woman of Canaan; or, Prayer Heard and Answered	1
5. St. Peter; or, the Zealous and Faithful Minister. Part II.	1	23. St. Thomas; or, Encouragement to the Weak Believer.	1
6. St. Matthew; or, Leaving all for Christ	1	24. Philip; or, the Heaven-sent Guide	1
7. Lazarus and his Sisters; or, the Family whom Jesus Loved	1	25. Timothy; or, in the Morning Sow thy Seed	1
8. Zaccheus; or, the Seeker Rewarded	1	26. Gallio; or, the Spirit of Careless Indifference	1
9. Mary; or, the Honoured Mother	1	27. Lydia; or, the Woman whose Heart the Lord opened	1
10. Judas Iscariot; or, a Traitor among the Twelve	1	28. The Heathen Jailor; or, What shall I do to be Saved?	1
11. Saul; or, the Pharisee Converted	1	29. The Man Born Blind; or, Christ near to us in the Hour of Need	1
12. St. Paul; or, the Soldier of Christ	1	30. Ananias and Sapphira; or the Hidden Falsehood brought to Light	1
13. Nicodemus; or, the Weak Believer made Strong	1	31. Simon the Sorcerer; or, the False Convert	1
14. Pilate; or, the Unrighteous Judge	1	32. Aquila and Priscilla; or, the Christian Helpers	1
15. The Dying Thief; or, Salvation to the Uttermost	1	33. The Cripple of Bethesda; or, Wilt thou be made Whole?	1
16. St. Stephen; or, the Fearless Martyr	1	34. Joseph of Arimathea; or, a Hidden One of Christ's Flock	1
17. The Woman who was a Sinner; or, the Penitent's Love to Christ	1		
18. Mary Magdalene; or, the Faithful Mourner at the Cross	1		

HATCHARDS, 187 PICCADILLY;

HAMILTON, ADAMS, & CO. 32 PATERNOSTER ROW, LONDON.

www.ingramcontent.com/pod-product-compliance
Lightning Source LLC
Chambersburg PA
CBHW020407030726
47496CB00007B/2348